THE
INCONSISTENT
WIDOW

Elizabeth Longrigg

Copyright © 2021 Elizabeth Longrigg

All rights reserved

ISBN-13: 9798719278124
ISBN-10: 1477123456

Cover design by: Mary Bowen
Library of Congress Control Number: 2018675309
Printed in the United States of America

To my neighbour

'Thou shalt love they neighbour as thyself'

Difficult but worth a try. Only don't overdo it!

CHAPTER 1

"My husband played rather a lot of golf, I really don't remember when he died."

This statement from the new tenant in the large Victorian Gothic house to the occupants of the other four flats, who were assembled in her sitting room, was met with a blank silence, as nobody could think of an appropriate response. The usual 'I'm sorry' murmured on hearing of a death was clearly unsuitable in this context. Two of the four other women had ex- husbands who were still alive, albeit remote from their present lives. One of these eventually broke the silence with a sound between a giggle and a snigger and the hostess, apparently content with the impact of her statement, went on to welcome them all and say that of course, having moved in as it were among them, she was anxious — indeed eager — to get to know them all.

"Now let me see if I get things right." She turned to the tallest of them, most like herself in build and colouring, but whose once red hair was laced with grey whereas her own was of a redness clearly maintained by artificial aid. "You're Marjorie, aren't you, and you live on the top floor in the flat above mine, and you're a retired academic so you're Dr - er - Dr..."

"Reed, Dr Marjorie Reed."

"Yes of course; I remember now. Dr Reed." She glanced at the wedding ring on the third finger of Marjorie's left hand and reflected briefly on the usefulness of a doctorate. She had it on good authority from one of Marjorie's colleagues that she had, in fact, never been married, but the title she had earned precluded the awkwardness of distinguishing between 'Miss' and 'Mrs' without resorting to the ambiguous 'Ms', which so often denoted a mistress rather than a wife, at least to the ears of their generation.

"But you must call me 'Marjorie', of course," the object of her covert scrutiny was saying.

"What do you like to be called yourself?" asked a woman as short and squat as the first two speakers were tall. "We only know you as 'Mrs Thorneycroft."

"Oh, you're Benedicta, aren't you? From the bottom flat; the 'garden flat' as estate agents call it."

"I call it the basement," Benedicta replied uncompromisingly. "It's all I can afford and it's quite good enough for an ex-nun, though I'm beginning to find the stairs down into it not so easy to manage. Good exercise, though."

'Mrs Thorneycroft' turned graciously from the

speaker to a small, thin, woman, who presented a somewhat shrivelled aspect, and remarked "You're on the floor above Benedicta, aren't you? I never know quite what to call it."

"I call it the *piano nobile*, and I'm Mary Ann Evans."

"How very interesting! The same name as George Eliot! Did your parents do that on purpose in the hope of your pursuing a literary career?"

"I blame my parents for a number of things, but that's not one of them. 'Evans' is my married name."

"Ah, so you're a widow, like me."

"Not as far as I know."

Mary Ann Evans did in fact know perfectly well that her ex was still alive as she regularly received a substantial amount of money from him, but she had been impressed by her hostess's conversation-stopping example and desirous of imitating her in indifference to the fate of husbands, ex or otherwise.

As she offered no further information the last guest now received the interested attention of her hostess, who had the ability to make her feel that far from being merely 'not least' she was the one saved till last as the most important and most interesting. "Now *you* must be Valerie Middleton!" Plump and not uncomely, dressed in large, loose-fitting garments of an indeterminately blue shade, Valerie was flattered to be the only one

4

whose full name was known and spoken, spoken moreover as if it belonged to somebody of significance. This was not lost on Benedicta, who gave credit for a very clever performance. 'This is a woman who knows how to manipulate people,' she thought. 'I'm the only one who's forestalled her, despite her flattering reference to my 'garden' flat. And it's interesting that she hasn't told us her given name. Why not, now? She can hardly expect us to go on calling her 'Mrs Thorneycroft'. Though come to think of it, we don't call people by name all that often. It's more in talking about them that names crop up, so it is.'

Her attention, and that of others who were not talking too much to notice, was caught by the sound of a key turning in the lock of the flat's main door, just across the narrow passage from the sitting room they were in. A tall, grey-haired man entered the room with the confidence of familiarity.

"Ah! At last! Now we can have a drink!" the hostess greeted him.

"Hullo, love; sorry I'm late. I'll open the bottles now." He disappeared into the kitchen, leaving the assembled company in very little doubt as to his relationship to the new tenant.

'Wow!' thought Valerie, whose time as main object of interest had been interrupted by the arrival, 'this must be the boyfriend. Who'd have thought it? At *her* age!'

The tall man reappeared bearing a tray laden with

half a dozen glasses and a bottle each of red and white wine, which he proceeded to pour very expertly in response to the preferences expressed by the guests.

"Oh, and there are some bits of food under those sheets of greaseproof in the kitchen." This sounded more like a command than a statement. In response to it he disappeared again, to return a few moments later with some rather attractive looking canapés. The hostess waved a graceful hand towards him and announced to the company in general "This is Theodore."

Marjorie Reed was the first to recover. "Hullo Ted," she said. "I know you from college, don't I? But not as 'Theodore'!"

"Oh, I've always called him 'Theodore'."

"Yes, I'm always called that here." The subject of the conversation gave a gratified smile.

"Well, whichever. Do you know anybody else or shall I introduce people?" Marjorie looked at the smile and considered fleetingly that perhaps he could have been attractive without it. She did the rounds of the introductions ending with Mary Ann Evans, over whom he towered by feet rather than inches.

"Which flat do you live in?" he enquired politcly.

"Oh, the *piano nobile*!" she replied, as if that should have been obvious. As Ted was a scientist rather than a linguist, however, he appreciated neither the meaning of the words nor their significance.

"Pardon?" was his only reply.

Valerie Middleton, who had observed this with some amusement, intervened to explain. "Oh, she always says that. She means the main floor, the one with bigger rooms and higher ceilings. I live on the next floor up, which is a *piano* much less *nobile*!"

Ted decided that Valerie was greatly preferable to Mary Ann and continued to talk to her. Their conversation hardly promised to be inspiring as it was initially about the weather. It emerged, however, that Ted had reason to be particularly interested in tomorrow's weather as he and his wife were having a barbecue in their garden for their daughter's 40th birthday.

Valerie blinked and wondered where the wife might be and where their hostess fitted into the picture. She decided to glean what information she could from Marjorie as soon as possible.

When the food seemed to be finished and it might look greedy to have any more to drink the inmates of the rest of the house departed from the new tenant's floor, leaving Ted to help, apparently, with the clearing up. Somehow they all seemed to gravitate towards Benedicta's flat, which was indeed the lowest, if by no means the largest, and the furthest away from the one they had been in. A discussion of the newly arrived occupant of the house, still known only as 'Mrs Thorneycroft' was too interesting a subject to be delayed and they all found their way to the unpretentious basement which housed Benedicta. Valerie had grabbed a bottle of white wine from her fridge on the way so there was no danger of dryness either literal or metaphorical.

"Well, what do you think?" Benedicta, as tenant of the flat, had the right to begin.

"She's an attractive woman," Marjorie ventured.

"The boyfriend certainly seems to think so!" Mary Ann sniffed.

"He's a married man who lives at home with his wife!" Valerie informed them.

"How do you know that?" Mary Ann asked in some surprise.

"He told me. They're having a party for their daughter's birthday tomorrow, or a barbecue or something. But you know him don't you Marjorie?"

"Yes, and I do know he's married. He's got rather a bad name in college for the way he behaves with women, especially young ones. People have been very sorry for his wife. But I wouldn't have thought....with this one......" Marjorie's words trailed indecisively and she took a thoughtful drink.

"What I can't understand is why she didn't tell us what to call her. I asked her straight out and she just never answered the question. Did you notice that?" Benedicta asked.

"The boyfriend only called her 'love', which was not much help," Valerie laughed.

"I really don't think you should call him that, it's not quite fair to her," Marjorie objected.

"Well, personally," Mary Ann interposed, "whatever else he is or may be, I think he's decidedly common." As that was so obviously what Mary Ann would think, though nobody said as much to her face, no importance was attached to it. After some repetitive circling round the subject and a realisation that nothing seemed likely to be gained by further discussion, they repaired to their several apartments to ponder the situation in solitude.

CHAPTER 2

The new tenant spent a profitable week having 'Theodore' hang pictures where she wanted them hung, put bookshelves against all available walls and install her computer and its necessary adjuncts. He was there at least once every day. The occupants of the other flats in the house spent an equally profitable week noting the fact. Only Valerie, while admitting that it added considerable spice to their lives, regarded other aspects of the situation as not entirely desirable, for Theodore always parked his car in *her* space in the house's car park. As 'residents only' parking was permitted on the street and non-residents had to use somewhat scarce parking permits, and as Valerie always kept her car outside on the road anyway, this was understandable. Still, it was annoying.

In the intervals between Theodore's visits, however, the earlier occupants of the house were not neglected. Benedicta was taken out to coffee; Marjorie to the theatre; Mary Ann to a concert and Valerie to a meal at Gee's accompanied by many apologies concerning the *unfortunately very necessary* parking of the car. She was slightly mollified, though not entirely forgiving of Theodore, with whom she had had one or two brusque exchanges about the matter.

There was another seemingly fortuitous gathering, this time over coffee which everybody seemed to have dropped in for, in the flat belonging to Benedicta, who made an announcement as the last to arrive settled down. "Rosario's away for the day; Theodore's driving her to Hampshire where she used to live before she came here to Oxford."

"What did you call her?" Marjorie enquired.

"Rosario. Why?"

"That's not her name," Marjorie declared decisively, "she's called Rosa."

"It's what she told me her name was," Benedicta responded with equal decidedness.

"Oh really," Mary Ann objected, "it can't be Rosario; that sounds so masculine."

"It means 'rosary'; it's a common enough name for Catholic girls, so it is, especially Spanish ones." Benedicta knew about such things.

"But surely she's not a Spanish Catholic!" Mary Ann objected. "She sounds totally English."

"Yes, she was born and brought up in Spain; but she never went to school and had an English governess." Marjorie was sure she knew best.

"She never mentioned that to me," Mary Ann mused, "but she told me to call her Rosalie. What did she say to you, Valerie?"

"I heard about the Spanish upbringing," Valerie replied, "but she said her name was Rosita. However she did say 'just call me Rose'."

"No wonder she didn't tell us her name the other evening," Benedicta mused. "She's told us all something different!"

"It's not so surprising," Marjorie was already regarding 'Rosa' as a particular friend and was quick to defend her, "lots of people have different versions of their name which different people use. My brother calls me Midge, or even 'Midget', which nobody else does, and come to think of it, all the people in a whole college know Ted and none of them call him 'Theodore'."

This explanation was reluctantly agreed to be not entirely unreasonable, but each of the women was privately convinced that she was the special one and had thus been told Ros/e/a/alie/ario/ita's favourite — or perhaps 'real' name. Eventually and unsurprisingly, however, they settled on the shortest version in general conversation, using the 'special' name with which they had, as it were, been privately entrusted, only when talking or writing to the recipient in private.

Benedicta appreciated the coffee for which she

had been taken by 'Rosario', but she was in no hurry to form any definite opinion about her. She was not unaware that the names chosen to impart to the other denizens of 'number nine' had been well suited to the disposition of each hearer. As an ex-nun she herself might well be expected to rejoice in a religious name like Rosario, while 'Rosita', though reinforcing the exotic Spanish background, would go down better with sensible Valerie when reduced to 'Rose'. She was not so sure about 'Rosa' for Marjorie, but 'Rosalie' was a very Mary Annish name. She'd known people who took care, when going to meet a friend, to wear the kind of clothes the friend would like and approve of. She'd never tried to do anything of the sort herself, but having worn a nun's habit for a number of years she was objectively interested in the way people dressed. 'The onlooker sees most of the game' she mused to herself as she pondered the fact that nuns could be very good onlookers if they belonged to an order which gave them contact with the outside world because they were very much regarded as non-participants.

Her thoughts were interrupted by the telephone. It was 'Rosario', who, as well as inviting Benedicta to go to tea with her in the Randolph Hotel in a couple of days' time, engaged in a lengthy and not uninteresting conversation about her trip to Hampshire to see her solicitor. At the end of it Benedicta rang off feeling far more inclined to be charitable in her judgment of the possible motive behind the multiple choice of names, though still puzzled by it.

She might have been slightly less charitable had she been able to hear the next phone call, this time to Marjorie, in which 'Rosa' begged her company to help alleviate her weariness and boredom, "because," Rose continued, "I've spent all yesterday and a good part of today with Theodore and he has absolutely no sense of humour and is just *so* boring that I really must have an antidote! Moreover he's cooked me a Chinese meal and I simply *hate* Chinese food so can you *please* come and eat it!"

"Well, I'm particularly fond of Chinese food, though I never cook it for myself, so that would be a treat. But I would have come anyway. Do you mean now?"

"Oh yes please; as soon as possible."

"I'll be there 'momentarily' as the Americans say." Marjorie merely combed her long, lustreless, not very ruly hair, wished she had the energy to do something else with it, and descended to Rose's flat. It was approached by a narrow, steep staircase between dun-coloured walls and was thinly clad in a brownish carpet. The landlords, an Oxford college, were clearly unwilling to devote any funds to improving its appearance. Marjorie had long since ceased to notice but it was something of a shock to the uninitiated visitor unused to the rigours of 'plain living, high thinking' Oxford. So thin was the stair carpet that approaching footsteps were clearly audible and Rose was at the open door to greet her guest.

"Oh, do come in; I'm so glad to see you. Let's have a drink while your Chinese meal heats up and then you can eat it while I peck at something else."

"Why don't you tell Ted, er - Theodore - you don't like Chinese?"

"Soft of me, I know, but I've left it too late. At first I didn't like to because he was so pleased to have produced such things, and I must admit it's very good of its kind; now I can't bring myself to admit that I've actually disliked it all along. I've tried hints, but I'm afraid he's impervious to those. You'll have gathered he's not what you'd call conversationally perceptive."

"But you see a lot of him, don't you?"

This could hardly be denied given the frequency with which Ted's very old and hence very noticeable car was to be seen in the house's car park.

Rose sighed. "I have to have a very definite reason to stop him coming, and even then he's very likely to want to come and help. And he *is* very helpful and very good at doing the sort of odd jobs one can hardly get anybody to do these days. But friends of mine have said to me that though he's an extremely useful person to have around I really must not let him control my life. He does just love looking after people. I'm not the only one, you know. He's got a friend who lives near them in Headington and he does a vast amount for her too."

"He can't have much time left over to spend at home."

"He spends Saturdays at home - well, usually; if I don't very particularly want something done or need taking somewhere. But what about you? You must have had men in your life. And of course you've been married, haven't you?"

"Well, yes and no."

Rose laughed. "I could say that about my marriage, but it would be strange if yours was very similar. Or were you a perpetual golf widow too?"

"No, I couldn't say that. He wasn't interested in golf, or sport of any kind, and in fact we never actually lived in the same house together, except for brief weekends or weeks, but nowadays we'd be considered 'partners'. He was a sort of lasting fiancé, lasting for quite a number of years. In fact I did seriously consider having a child by him and bringing it up on my own. I even told my parents as much. I'm afraid they were horrified. But as nothing happened after a number of what you might call conjugal visits I finally gave up. He gradually slipped out of my life. Neither of us ever married. I've had several subsequent relationships, all equally brief and unsatisfactory. I've found teaching and writing and the companionship of compatible women preferable to having men in my life, though of course some of them do have their uses, like your Ted."

"Oh, you mustn't call him 'my' Ted, or even my

Theodore. He's not my lover, you know."

"No?"

"NO! Definitely not! I would call him my *cavalier servente*, only people don't understand such a term these days,"

"They will do if they've read Kipling, surely."

"Does anybody nowadays? Apart from the children's books, of course. I've read them myself, *Plain Tales from the Hills* and *Hill Tales from the Plain* and so on, though you know I'm totally uneducated, I never even went to school; but I have read a lot. I never met anybody in Hampshire who'd read them, however."

"Well," Marjorie was pleased to say, "you might be pleasantly surprised in Oxford. Quite a lot of people read such things here."

"That would certainly be pleasant to find. Our Hampshire acquaintances were mainly interested in shooting pheasants and going to point-to-points and of course having dinner parties, and really I care for none of these things. In fact that's the main reason why I came to live in Oxford; though of course the old country house we lived in was much too big for me, anyway."

"I can see you've got a good deal of rather large furniture," Marjorie remarked, looking round the heavily furnished room with its overabundance of dark, old-fashioned, chairs, tables, cupboards and an exceedingly uncomfortable-looking sofa, mainly consisting of sooty coloured wood. "And you do seem to have a vast number of books!" she added, to avoid expressing any opinion on the furniture.

"Oh, there are boxes and boxes of them that haven't been unpacked yet; but there's really nowhere to put them now. I can't bear to part with any of them."

"Well, I can understand that."

"You see, I did originally intend to buy a house in Oxford, but they're terribly expensive if they're anywhere central, and I want to be able to go to the theatre and so on without having to travel miles to get there. And it's not as if I can have Theodore take me to anything like that: he never goes to a play, detests opera, sings in a church choir but never goes to concerts."

"Well, I'd be very happy to go with you; I very much enjoy all those things."

"Oh, dear Marjorie; I was so hoping that would be the case. I *am* glad to have come here and met you!"

Marjorie basked in her new friend's approval and they arranged to go to a play the very next week. She left the flat in an unusually happy state of mind - besides being internally fortified by a particularly delicious (and free) Chinese dinner.

CHAPTER 3

Benedicta, ready and waiting for 'Rosario' to take her out to tea, was more than a little surprised to hear a male voice calling "Hullo...o...o!" from the steep staircase down to her basement flat. It was Theodore/Ted and he was carrying the shopping she'd had delivered from the Co-op. She'd known it was there, it had arrived while she was changing to go out, but she'd decided to take it down in stages when she came back from tea, because this operation always took some time. For one of her advanced years it would necessitate at least three trips and the probable transference of some items to extra bags. The packers at the shop had no difficulty with an accumulation of heavy objects, but she would have to see to it that each bag was of no more than manageable weight.

"Theodore!" she cried as she watched him descend the stairs holding three bulging bags, "aren't you just the kindest! But how did you get in?"

"Rose told me where to find your hidden key. I wanted to save you an extra trip up these stairs.

She's waiting for you in the car. Just come out when you're ready. I'll put the key back."

He dumped the shopping on the floor of the minute kitchen, seeming to know by instinct where it was, and disappeared up the stairs before Benedicta could gather her outdoor clothes and put them on. Pleased though she was to have what was to her a considerable task performed so easily, she found the uninvited invasion of her space a little disturbing. She immediately scolded herself for ingratitude and lack of charity, but the feeling would not quite go away.

Halfway down the drive was Rose's car with Rose sitting in the back seat. Theodore reached it just a little ahead of Benedicta and held open the door of the front passenger seat for her.

"I'm going to drop you both at the Randolph," he informed her, "as there's really nowhere to park anywhere near and Rose can't walk too far. Her back's bad again. She can ring me on her mobile when you're ready to come home and I'll pick you up."

"This is luxury indeed, so it is! I'd never a thought about how we'd get there. I can still take a bus myself. Hullo, Rose. I would have gone in the back seat, I'm nowhere near as tall as you are."

"Well, on the way back perhaps. I managed to get in here though I might be very slow getting out. But then I go in the front all the time and I wanted you to enjoy it. I know we were able to walk to the

Crèperie for our little lunch, but it's not exactly luxurious and it's too noisy to talk comfortably. All those bare tables and scraping chairs!"

The journey to the Randolph took only a few minutes. Theodore got out of the car to help Rose unbend herself from the back seat, shook his fist and mouthed insults at a driver who honked impatiently behind them, (Rose was not able to move quickly), opened the door for Benedicta and saw them both safely up the steps before getting into the car again.

The tea was a great success. There were delicious scones with jam and cream, cakes that tasted nearly as attractive as they looked, and a kindly waitress, more homely than their surroundings, who willingly supplied them with more hot water. The lofty-ceilinged room with its carpeted quietness and total lack of hustle and bustle conveyed a sense of there being plenty of time as well as plenty of space. Benedicta sank back into the sofa and remarked that it was very restful and quite a contrast with her flat. "I do feel pampered," she continued, "I lead quite a busy life, I do, what with going to Blackfriars most days; sitting in the lodge, working in their library."

"It must be rather like being a nun again, isn't it?"

"No, I wouldn't say that, but it's truly shown me how very different it is being a monk! Well, not a monk, a friar. But most people wouldn't know the meaning of that. I expect you do though, you lived in Spain and you must be a Catholic with a name like Rosario."

"Yes, though my mother only became a Catholic when she married."

"Oh, she wasn't Spanish, then? I thought you don't seem very Spanish yourself."

"I suppose that accounts for it. Of course, I had an English governess and I didn't go to school and mix with local children."

"Were you an only child?"

"I haven't any family. I lost my mother early."

"But you were brought up a Catholic? You don't go to Mass, do you." The last sentence was a statement, not a question. The residents of number nine, as the Victorian Gothic house was generally known, were not unaware of one another's comings and goings.

"Well, I do sometimes, but I don't seem to have got into the way of it since I've been here. I don't like the Oratory and I don't like getting up early. I seem to take most of the morning."

"There's a Sunday evening mass at Blackfriars; why don't you come to that with me?"

"Well, I may just do that. Ask me again. But now, tell me about yourself. Is your name really Benedicta or was that the name you took in the convent?"

"It is my baptismal name, in fact. I was in more than one convent and had more than one religious name — but only one at a time!" Benedicta could not resist adding the last phrase, but Rose (or whatever) was either unaware of the implied reference to herself or determined to take no notice of it.

"More than one convent?" she queried in reply. "How was that?"

"I couldn't seem to find my true vocation; I even tried the Poor Clares, and we *were* poor. We used to go to the market in the evenings and sweep up the day's leavings and then take them and use what we could."

"That does seem to be rather off-puttingly extreme!"

"Yes, perhaps, but it was doing without any intellectual life that really put me off. I'm too independent minded, so I am. I left the convent and went for school teaching."

"You seem very intellectual to poor, uneducated me," Rose sighed, "with all you do for Blackfriars and one of the colleges. Do tell me more about it."

Benedicta was by no means averse to describing her intellectual interests at some length and was listened to with flattering attention until she herself realised that she had been perhaps rather carried away by her own enthusiasm and too inclined to launch into a monologue, greatly though she had relished the opportunity. Rose protested that she found it all unusually interesting and just the kind of thing she had come to Oxford to hear, then summoned the waitress, paid the bill and telephoned Theodore on her mobile. They were waiting for him on the steps when he drew up outside the hotel and both were eager to tell him that they had enjoyed an exceptionally pleasant tea. Arrived back at number nine Theodore insisted on seeing Benedicta into her flat before parking the car and taking Rose into hers. It was of course noted by the other occupants of the house that his own car stayed in its — usurped — place in the car park.

Some hours later Mary Ann telephoned Valerie. "I see his car's still here!" she announced with little preamble.

Valerie had no need to ask whose. "Yes," she replied, "in *my* space as usual!"

"I think I've just remembered where I've seen him before," Mary Ann continued. "I knew he looked somehow familiar but I couldn't place him. Now I've got an idea that he sings in the choir of the church I go to."

"I didn't know you went to church." Valerie was surprised.

"Not very often, certainly. But there's one I go to sometimes on a Sunday evening. It's got quite a good choir. That must be where I've seen him. He's tall enough to be noticeable. Anyway, I'll go again so I can find out."

"I'm sure that's as good a reason as any!"

"They have drinks at the back of the church after the service. I've never stayed for that before but I will this time. I don't suppose you'd like to come with me?"

"No, thank you. I've seen quite enough of that man in *our* car park and the thought of seeing him unnecessarily is *not* an incentive to go to church! But do tell me about it when you've been."

Valerie had more behind her dislike of Theodore than the usurped car space though she would not have admitted it willingly. She was disinclined to be tolerant of erring husbands as her own had had the classic affair with his secretary, which had eventually resulted in his leaving the marital home and asking for a divorce. It had all happened a long time ago but the bitterness of it had unsurprisingly disposed Valerie to despise men in general and adulterous ones in particular. She was immensely tempted to ring Rose and demand that Theodore move his car so that she could put hers in its rightful place. "That'll interrupt their little games!" she said to herself with a smirk of satisfaction. After deliberating for some time she found the number and dialled it. To her disappointment — and surprise — it was engaged. "Hmph!" she muttered. "I seem to have been wrong about that. Oh well! Probably a good thing. People living in the same house need to get on with one another. No point in making an enemy of Rose, however I may feel about *him.*"

CHAPTER 4

In a modern, somewhat utilitarian Close in Headington, Millie Gatward was on a step-ladder cleaning the tops of her kitchen cupboards prior to rearranging the ornaments which usually adorned them, plus a new one, whose acquisition had necessitated this extra work. A key was heard to turn in the Yale lock of the front door. Millie continued to wipe the cupboard tops as she called out "Hullo Ted!"

"Hullo love," was the immediate reply as Ted made the only two paces necessary to bring him from the front door to the kitchen. "Oh, you should let me do that, love! I'd hardly need the ladder!"

"You wouldn't know where to put the things. But you can hand them up to me if you like."

"Can't we have our gin and tonic first? I'm a bit later than usual. I had to get a lot of things for Rose."

"This won't take any time now I've finished cleaning."

"Oh, all right. Really, those cupboards should go

all the way to the ceiling. Then you wouldn't have to clean the tops."

"I wouldn't be able to reach things on the top shelves. Anyway, I like having pretty things on top. Makes the kitchen look less clinical."

"Our cupboards go to the ceiling and our kitchen doesn't look clinical!"

"You can say that again. Your kitchen hasn't been decorated since you moved in thirty years ago." Millie placed the last ornament and came down to floor level. Ted was already getting out the glasses and the tonic. It was Saturday and on Saturday afternoons he went shopping in Waitrose not only for Rose but for the supper he was going to cook at home. On the way back he stopped off at Millie's to fortify himself with a gin and tonic and the kind of conversation to which the home environment was not conducive. He was greatly given to habit and routine.

They settled to their drinks in the 'lounge', side by side on the sofa as Ted liked to sit.

"I don't know why you had to get this new sofa," he grumbled. "I liked the other one better and it looked pretty new anyway."

"It was old-fashioned," Millie objected.

"You shouldn't get rid of things because you think they're old-fashioned. Rose has got nothing but old-fashioned things. So have we, come to that."

"That's your choice. But it's not the way I like

things."

"If you get things new they're old-fashioned before long anyway. Old things just stay old."

"If they don't get eaten up by woodworm; not to mention grubby and worn out. But I don't have to furnish my house the way *you* like it. What are you going to cook tonight?"

"Bouillabaisse. Emily likes that. As long as I don't put shellfish in it. She doesn't like shellfish. I'll bring you some tomorrow. I always make too much"

The conversation was following an established route. It varied little from one such session to another. There was a comfortable sameness about it occasionally enlivened by something out of the ordinary, as was in fact the case this time.

"There's a new verger coming to the church," Ted announced portentously, "and it's not a man, it's a lady; quite young, only in her thirties. She's going to live in that little house beside the parish rooms." Ted grinned and gave a happily anticipatory chuckle and added "I'll have to chat her up, won't I?"

"I don't know about 'have to'," Millie replied tolerantly, "but I've no doubt you will."

"Yes, I'm looking forward to meeting her. She'll be there tomorrow. You should come and meet her too."

"Not tomorrow. I've got to go to our parish church

tomorrow. I might come another time."

The second gins finished and nothing more note-worthy added to the conversation, Ted departed to begin on the bouillabaisse for himself and Emily. Millie went back into the kitchen, looked at the newly placed ornaments with a critical eye and got the ladder out again to rearrange them.

Ted drove up the unkempt drive to his own house and hoisted his shopping into the kitchen, whose low ceiling was dark with the accumulated cooking fumes of at least thirty years. The one window into the back garden and driveway gave little light. He was sitting at the large, heavy, wooden table skinning and cutting fish when his wife Emily appeared at the kitchen door.

"Oh, you're back," she observed.

"Yes, I've been back for a while."

"What are we having tonight?"

"Bouillabaisse."

"Oh good. I like that. As long as there aren't any shellfish in it."

"Yes, I know."

Emily disappeared again into the bowels of the house and Ted applied himself to the skinning and cutting up of raw fish with concentrated diligence. When everything was prepared to his satisfaction he carefully poured himself a gin and tonic, took it and his cigarettes into the garden, where a light, drizzly rain was beginning to make itself felt, went into the coal shed and pressed a button on his mobile phone. Millie, sitting in front of the gas fire in her lounge, reached for the remote control with one hand as she stood up and took the necessary few steps to the telephone, whose receiver she picked up with the other hand. "Hullo Ted," she said as she heard the clink of ice against a glass and the exhalation of a breath, "enjoying your fag and gin in the garden shed?"

There was the sound of another breath before the answer came. "Hullo, love; yes, thanks."

"How's the bouillabaisse going?"

"All right; I've cut everything up."

"What are you having with it?"

"Mashed potatoes and celeriac. I'll bring some round to you tomorrow."

The conversation, if such it could be called, proceeded along similar lines until Ted finally said "see you tomorrow," and rang off. Millie turned up the sound on the television and returned to her seat.

Some twenty minutes later the telephone rang once and then stopped. As the programme she was watching had lapsed into a commercial break, Millie got up and dialled 1471. Ted's mobile number was announced. She pressed 3 to ring it. As she had expected it was engaged. "I thought so," she murmured, "he pressed the wrong button, realised it wasn't the one he wanted and stopped it immediately. I wonder who he's ringing now; Rose, I expect, or one of those girls from the college." She gave a very slight sigh and used the rest of the commercial break to pour herself a drink.

On Sunday morning Ted arrived at the church of his choice rather earlier than usual. He was interested to meet the new woman verger. His wife Emily was already there. She'd long grown tired of waiting for Ted to drive into town late, as he usually did, so she always went independently by bus. She was a churchwarden and took the responsibilities of this position with characteristic seriousness.

The new verger was easily spotted as she was wearing a traditional black cassock-like garment. The organist, a dominant-looking woman of Junoesque proportions, was talking to her as Ted bore down on them with the purposeful step he was inclined to use when approaching a new interest. He took no notice of the organist, who was not a favourite of his, bur bared his teeth in a predatory grin at the verger. The organist, not a woman to be easily overlooked, intervened. "Oh Ted, this is our new verger, Bettine Bartlett."

"Call me Bee," the object of these attentions responded with a winning smile. "I'm always called Bee."

"Oh, that's nice, Bee. It really suits you somehow.

You're living in the little old house beside the church hall, aren't you; I've always wanted to see inside that house."

"Well then, you must come and see me and I'll show you round."

"I'd really like that" - another grin. "When can I come?"

"Any time. I don't know anybody here yet."

The organist, Clarissa Hillman, totally left out of the conversation, gave something like a snort and went to muster the choir and check the tidiness of the choirboys. She was more popular with them than with the choir men, whom she treated in much the same way. The boys appreciated her concern and fairness, the men were inclined to resent it. One, however, Cedric Adams, a countertenor, who was unashamedly camp and probably the most musically able member of the choir, regarded himself as 'on her side' and something like a friendship existed between them.

"Hullo, Clarry," he greeted her, "met the new verger yet?"

"Yes, have you?"

"No, I've been here in the vestry. What's she like?"

"Short, fat, plain and sexy."

Cedric giggled. "Darling - you're so acerbic! I love it!"

Ted was still engaged in eager conversation with Bee when Mary Ann Evans opened the heavy door of the church and looked round to see what she needed to pick up in the way of hymn and prayer books. She saw Ted and decided to ask his advice as an excuse to find out who he was so eagerly talking to. 'Obviously not his wife,' she immediately concluded with the knowledgeable sourness of a divorcee. She approached him purposefully and greeted him. "Good morning, Theodore."

Bee gave a chortle, made a face and said "Theodore! Is that your name?"

"Yes, but most people call me Ted."

"Rose always calls you Theodore!" Mary Ann objected in somewhat proprietary tones.

"Who's Rose?" Bee enquired.

"Well, um, she lives in the same house as this lady - er, um - ." It being obvious that he had forgotten her name Mary Ann graciously supplied it: "Mary Ann Evans."

"I'm Bee," was the response. "I'm new here."

"Oh? Where are you from?" Mary Ann was guessing Birmingham or Manchester, but she was wrong.

"Dunmow," was the reply. "It's in Essex."

"Yes, of course; one knows of Dunmow. It's the place where a flitch of bacon is given each year to the couple who haven't had a quarrel in twelve months."

"Oh, you know about that. Not that I've ever qualified. I've got two ex-husbands."

"At your age? You can't be more than forty at the

most!"

"No, I'm thirty-five. Oh, there's the organ starting up. I'll talk to you when we're having coffee after the service."

Mary Ann found a space halfway down the aisle. It was not difficult; none of the pews was full. Clarissa Hillman wound the introductory voluntary to a close and embarked on the melody of the first hymn. The congregation disentangled their feet from the kneelers, which should have been hanging from the backs of the pews but were mainly on the floor, stood up in an uneven progression and began to sing the first line of the hymn as the choir filed in, making quite enough noise to drown all but the most blatantly forceful members of the congregation.

A number of years at a rigidly traditional Anglican girls' boarding school had left Mary Ann with a considerable knowledge of hymns so she could easily sing Onward Christian Soldiers quite accurately while thinking of something completely different. She had not previously given any thought to after service coffee, but as she was finding the assembled personnel considerably more interesting than she had imagined possible, she found herself deciding that it might be rather a good idea, which she implemented as the organ was playing the voluntary after the final hymn.

It was a little difficult to talk to Bee as all the regular parishioners wanted to meet her and Theodore was in perpetual attendance, bringing her cups of coffee and telling her the names and functions of all comers who were not quick enough to introduce themselves. Mary Ann watched with interest as she absorbed this usefully available information. Among others Emily came up and murmured rather shyly: "Hullo, I'm Emily." Then turning to her husband, who was still stationed protectively beside Bee, she asked: "Will you be coming home for lunch, Ted?"

"Oh, I don't know; I haven't decided. There's a lot left over from last night."

"Yes, I know. I'll be eating it all week from the look of it. Though I suppose you'll be giving some to Millie."

"Yes, I said I would."

Emily turned away and went to talk to the other churchwarden. Bee and Mary Ann were both staring in disbelief.

"Was that your wife?" Bee asked, in tones that implied more astonishment than interrogation. Ted appeared to be unaware of her tone or to infer nothing from it.

'Yes, that's Emily," he replied casually, "she's a churchwarden. Now how about me coming to have a look at your house?"

"What now?"

"When you're ready. I'll see you home anyway."

"It's not a hundred yards away!"

"All the better. Do you want to change out of your cassock?"

"No, I wore it to come here. It's better than a coat."

Ted took her arm and steered her out of the church. Mary Ann stood staring after them.

"Well!" she said aloud.

The organist, Clarissa, accompanied by Cedric Adams, came up behind her. "Well indeed!" she declared, in tones of agreement. "Or more probably *not* well!"

Mary Ann turned to her as to an authority: "Whatever does his wife think?" she asked. They looked over to where Emily was talking to a stern-looking man, who could have been any age between sixty and seventy-five.

"Whatever she thinks she doesn't give anything away. She's used to it, of course. He's usually chatting up some member of the congregation, and she occasionally laughs. But then everybody thinks it's a joke. This looks a bit different."

Somewhat belatedly Clarissa and Mary Ann exchanged names and basic information about themselves. The circumstances of their meeting had produced a mutual sense of affinity. They had an extra cup of coffee together and continued their conversation, which ended with the expressed intention of meeting again the following Sunday. Mary Ann walked back to her flat elated with the thought of all the interesting information she had acquired and the pleasurable anticipation of imparting it to the other occupants of the house. She debated whether to telephone them individually or merely invite one, or perhaps two, to tea and let them spread the word to the others. She pondered on this as she sat at a table in the window eating her rather elegant lunch of smoked salmon, caviar and a carefully mixed salad. From this vantage point she saw Ted/Theodore walking over the gravel of the drive. He had presumably left his car in the road for once as it was Sunday and there was no embargo on parking by non- residents. It was already after two o'clock. This unusual lateness — he was usually to be seen on his way to Rose's flat by one o'clock, if not twelve thirty — added interest to the news Mary Ann was eager to impart and she soon decided that Valerie was the most suitable recipient. Benedicta's Catholic scruples made her regard gossip as a form of detraction and therefore a sin. Marjorie was so intent on regarding herself as Rose's best friend that she was inclined to think favourably of anybody connected with her. Valerie, on the other hand, was already anti-Theodore because of his appropriation of her car space. She was, moreover, like Mary Ann, a divorcee with little sympathy for straying husbands, having suffered from one herself. Mary Ann dialled Valerie's number.

"Hullo," came the answering voice, "oh hullo Mary

Ann. I've been wondering if I'd hear from you. Did you go to that church this morning?"

"I did indeed, and it was *most* interesting!"

"I thought you were going in the evening."

"I used to, but then I decided the morning would be a better time."

"A better time to worship or a better time to see people?"

"Well, both really. Anyway, I did see people."

"Tell me all!"

"Come down and have a cup of coffee with me. It'll take too long over the telephone."

"I'll be there *now.*"

So for the next hour or more Valerie was regaled with a detailed description and discussion of Theodore's behaviour with the new verger; his wife's reaction, or lack of it; the significant failings of men in general and Theodore in particular.

"So what's she like then, this Bee?" Valerie enquired. "Is she like Rose at all?"

"Oh no, quite the opposite; she could hardly be more unlike: short, fat, with a common-looking round face, you know, no sort of *bone* structure." Mary Ann's own features, though small, were bony in a way that she herself considered aristocratic, though most people merely considered them sharp. "I couldn't see what she was wearing, of course, she was in a long black garment, like the verger in *Dad's Army.*"

"No, really? I didn't realise anybody still wore such things. And what's the wife like?"

"Oh, very different; thin, no bust, almost concave. Stands as if she's trying to hide the fact that she's got a bosom at all."

"Mousy, is she?"

"Not exactly. She's fairly tall. I never think tall people can be mousy, do you? She's very sweet looking."

"She must be very tolerant, anyway."

"Ridiculously so, in my opinion. Now I come to think of it she even asked her husband if he'd be taking some of their last night's supper to 'Millie'. And he said he would. His wife didn't seem to mind."

"Well," Valerie pondered on this information. "I suppose she may think there's safety in numbers. He's less likely to leave her if he's got three of them than if there was only one."

"That might depend," Mary Ann observed, seeing a chance to air her Italian, "on who's *la favorita,* and also if they know about each other; not to mention if any of them actually *wants* him for herself. Rose might be in with a chance if she does, but actually she's never very nice about him. She often complains about him being 'too controlling', as she puts it."

"Yes, I've heard that. She's very willing to make use of him, though. Marjorie says he often cooks for her."

"He's a bit late for lunch today; unless of course he's given *her* some of last night's supper too!"

CHAPTER 5

Several Sundays passed. Mary Ann Evans was now a notably regular attender at church and had formed a considerable friendship with the organist, Clarissa Hillman. They even went out for tea in the middle of the week. Mary Ann would have preferred lunch, but as Clarissa always collected her in her car and took her to Woodstock or somewhere similar, she was by no means averse to accompanying her. Clarissa was particularly partial (as she expressed it) to a cream tea with scones. They were served two each and, as one was enough for Mary Ann, Clarissa would have three of them. With such an arrangement they were both very happy, though Mary Ann winced slightly at this use of the word 'partial'. As, however, Clarissa attended more services, as well as choir practices, in the church she was a better source of information than anybody else and thus decidedly worth cultivating, despite occasional infelicities in the use of language.

"So how have things been at number nine?" Clarissa enquired.

"Well, there has been something of a falling off in

the number of Theodore's attendances lately. He does go most afternoons but not so many lunch times, and he doesn't seem to stay so long."

"That's not too surprising. Bee's church-sitting most lunch times and he goes in to be with her. Sometimes they leave early and it looks as if they go out to lunch together."

"Does he take her in his car?"

"Not that anybody's seen. They either walk off somewhere or go in her car."

"Oh, she's got a car, has she?"

"Oh yes, very recognisable; it's got a number plate with BEE on it!"

"How very vulgar!" exclaimed Mary Ann, predictably.

"Apparently it was a present from her second husband."

"Clever of her to keep it!"

"She often talks about him and he comes to Oxford sometimes---and even *stays* with her!"

"Hmph!" Mary Ann sniffed contemptuously. "I can't say I'd want that to happen with my ex! It makes you wonder why they got divorced."

"She's got somebody else who comes and stays sometimes; a much older man. He came to Even-song once and she introduced him all round. It was very funny. Cedric — you know Cedric, very camp — said 'Oh, is this your father? Or an uncle, perhaps?' He did it on purpose, of course. It was quite obvious that the chap was, as Bee hastily claimed, her 'current bloke'."

"Oh dear! She really is *very* common, isn't she! But then of course so is Theodore, so he wouldn't notice."

"I'm afraid quite a number of other people in the parish do, though. It is North Oxford, after all. But to do them justice, they're more disapproving of the way Ted runs round after her and waits on her hand foot and finger than anything else. His wife Emily's a really nice woman and everybody feels embarrassed by her husband's behaviour and sorry for *her*."

"Well, there's not a great deal I can say for my ex," Mary Ann observed as she poured herself a second cup of tea, "but he was sufficiently well bred to behave very properly in public. He never said or did anything to draw attention to himself. He was just cold and distant and inattentive at home, when he was there, which wasn't very often."

"You don't really miss him, then."

"I can't say I do. I was more surprised than upset when he left and wrote saying he wanted a divorce so that he could marry somebody else. Apparently she'd been his mistress for some years. I'd thought he was too cold to care much for anybody. I can't think what she sees in him, apart from his money. I must admit he's not ungenerous when it comes to large amounts, though he did tend to go round turning lights off and complaining that the heating was turned up too high. I used to think it was for something to do and say."

"Oh yes; mine does that too. It's just a control thing. They all have that in some way or other."

"I don't suppose Rose's late husband did," Mary Ann mused. "She says he was always out playing golf and she never saw him at all. I suppose that's why she complains about Theodore being so controlling: she's not used to it."

"Well, Bee doesn't seem to mind," Clarissa laughed through a mouthful of scone number three and sent a barrage of crumbs over the table, "she gazes at him gooey-eyed and laps it all up."

Mary Ann suppressed a shudder at her informant's table manners and made a sign to the waitress that she was ready to pay the bill. Enough was, after all, enough and she had gleaned a useful amount of information with which to regale the other occupants of number nine.

Over the following weekend Rose had a friend staying with her and Theodore was totally absent. Indeed, Rose herself was hardly to be seen. Nobody in number nine was invited to meet 'Rachel', who had merely been mentioned in previous conversations as 'a very old and dear friend from Hampshire'. Certainly they spent a good deal of time out in Rose's or in Rachel's car. The visitor, therefore, acquired something of the status of a mystery woman in the eyes of the other inhabitants of the house, which enhanced rather than diminished the prestige of her hostess.

As Theodore/Ted was not in attendance on Rose it might have been expected that Millie would benefit by rather more of his company. There was, however, a falling off in the number of his telephone calls to her — down from half a dozen a day to one, if any — which was due to his frequent consorting with Bee. Millie suspected that this might be the case and determined to meet the new attraction. She therefore telephoned Ted herself and declared her intention of coming to the morning service at the church he attended, as he had earlier suggested that she should. His response was unabashed.

"Oh yes, what a good idea. Then you can meet Bee."

"That would be nice."

"I'm taking her for a drink after the service; you can come too."

"Thanks; that's kind."

Ted called in at Millie's on his way home from the usual Saturday shopping trip and arranged to pick her up the next morning at about ten o'clock for the ten-thirty service. Millie prepared herself for this occasion with some care. Though some half dozen or so years older than Ted she was still a good-looking woman with a healthy complexion, a well-rounded figure and a remarkably unwrinkled neck and cleavage, which she was not averse to showing. When she and Ted went through the heavy door into the church on Sunday morning, Mary

Ann Evans was already there, having arrived early for a preliminary interchange with her friend Clarissa. Bee was not yet to be seen and Ted was not particularly anxious to speak to anybody else so contented himself with settling Millie into a pew before going into the vestry, passing Cedric as he did so. Cedric sashayed up to Clarissa and Mary Ann and gave the former a kiss on the cheek.

"Hullo darling; how are we this morning? Have you seen who I've seen just settled into a pew? That's girlfriend number one or two, isn't it? Or has she been relegated to three now. I wonder what she'll make of the new number one!"

"She's probably seen a succession of them by all accounts," Clarissa answered. "He tends to like to show them off."

"It's really most unfair," Cedric complained in aggrieved tones, "if my sort go about with a number of young friends everybody says nasty things about us."

"Plenty of people say nasty things about Ted, I can assure you."

"I can vouch for that," Mary Ann nodded as she spoke. "There's a great deal of talk about him where I live because he's there almost every day seeing our newest tenant."

"Is he indeed?!" Cedric was interested. "However does he manage to find time for them all? And what number would *she* be?"

"I did think she was *la favorita,* number one," Mary Ann was pleased to be included in the conversation, "but she seems to have been displaced. Mind you, she's got a friend staying with her at the moment so she's hardly available."

"That might account for the presence of number — well, let's say three, today. But I must go; duty calls. See you after the service." Clarissa swept away to attack the organ with her usual vigour.

After the service Ted shepherded Millie into the back of the church and made a considerable play of introducing her to Bee, whom she greeted with a kind show of something like affection. "I'm so pleased to meet you; I've heard ever such a lot about you."

"All good things, I hope," Bee answered predictably.

"Oh, of course, all good things. Ted's always very kind, isn't he?"

Bee gave a snide little laugh "Well you could call it that!"

Ted gave a large grin, put an arm round Bee and another on to Millie's neck and steered them both to the door.

Clarissa and Mary Ann watched this charade

with undisguised interest. "Nobody seems to have asked Emily if she'd like to go with them," Clarissa remarked.

"Emily? Oh, his wife. Where is she?" Mary Ann scanned the dwindling congregation. "Probably in the kitchen area at the back. She's very good at keeping out of the way."

"Poor thing; she must be so embarrassed. I don't know how she stands the shame."

"Well, I know I couldn't," Clarissa replied forcibly. "I simply wouldn't put up with that sort of treatment."

"What would you do?"

"Tell that girl to take her hands off him for a start and tell him he was coming home with me or if he didn't he needn't come home at all."

Mary Ann swept a sideways glance at Clarissa's large and powerful form and murmured that she could quite believe it. "But I fear poor Emily hasn't your stature — or your confidence. Still, at least he's with two of them, if that makes it any better. I wonder how they're all getting on."

"Why don't we go and see?" Clarissa's eyes brightened. "You'd like a drink at the nearest pub, wouldn't you?"

"Now that," Mary Ann replied brightly, "is a very good idea!"

So they went the short distance to the Royal Oak and found themselves a table which commanded a good view of the inside of the pub without being too conspicuous. Mary Ann insisted on going up to get the drinks. "Nobody'll notice me," she said. "We don't want them to realise we're here."

"No, I'm sure they wouldn't appreciate our presence. They might even feel they should ask us to join them."

From the bar Mary Ann had a very good view of the trio under observation and certainly none of them noticed her. Bee was in fact talking in such a loud voice and commanding so much attention that a good many people were listening to her and to nobody else. She was regaling Millie with her life history and dwelling lengthily on the fact that she had two ex- husbands, the second of whom she still saw quite often when she wasn't with her 'current bloke'. She was clutching Ted's arm from time to time as she spoke and he was grinning as if with pride. Millie's expression could be described only as bland. Mary Ann took the drinks to the table where Clarissa was trying to look inconspicuous. Bee was still audible even from there.

"I've heard her go on about her severed spouses before," Clarissa observed, "but not quite so flamboyantly. I wonder how much she's had to drink!"

"She can't have had time to have much, unless she was topped up before the service."

"Maybe she's been having a go at the communion wine. I believe it's really strong stuff!"

Bee's voice was still to be heard almost without

cessation as she enumerated the number of different jobs she'd had and the number of operations,
including a hysterectomy "because Gary and me
didn't want any children."

She was still talking when Clarissa and Mary Ann
finished their drinks and left the pub.

CHAPTER 6

Rose's friend Rachel continued her stay at number nine and Bee's 'current bloke' took up residence in her picturesque house for the best part of a week so that Ted was virtually banished from both. Millie was therefore able to benefit from his attentions and was not sorry to do so as she had developed a nasty fluey cold and needed to keep to her bed. She was able to do this because Ted did all her shopping and put it away in the right places, filled her hot water bottle, made delicate meals and took them up to her. He had already seen to it that she had a telephone extension in her bedroom: he'd bought it for her and installed it some months earlier. Whenever he left her it was with strict instructions to ring him at any time if she needed anything. When he finally departed in the evening Millie sat up in bed sipping the very comforting hot drink of lemon, honey and brandy he'd given her and pondering on his kindness. It was almost worth being ill, she reflected, to be so pampered and looked after. The combination of these happy thoughts and the glow induced by the hot brandy made her feel sleepy and she put the almost empty cup on the table and the extra pillow on the floor and lay down comfortably.

She was just dozing off to sleep when the strident ringing of the telephone jerked her awake. It was Ted asking how she was. Repressing the desire to tell him that a telephone call was the last thing she needed she tactfully praised the quality of the hot drink and thanked him for all the help and kindness. She did finish the conversation by saying "I think I'll be able to sleep now," in the hope that this might prevent him from ringing again. As she put the receiver down she briefly considered the option of leaving it off the hook for the night, but she feared that if Ted were to ring several times to hear only the engaged signal he would have awful visions of her having had something happen to her, which would prompt him to come round immediately whatever the hour. She gave a sigh as she regretted her now wakeful state and pondered on past experience, which intruded on her previous contentment with the realisation that Ted always managed to render his kindness less gratifying by doing just too much.

Rose's friend Rachel went home to Hampshire, Millie recovered her health, Ted resumed his attentions to Bee, whose 'current bloke' had returned to his home and his occupation in Essex. As Rose needed a good many things in her flat to be

unpacked, put up, taken down, mended or otherwise attended to, Ted was quite significantly busy.
He still managed to help Benedicta carry her delivered shopping down her steep staircase and
give useful advice to Marjorie about her ailing
computer, even offering to install a new printer
for her when she bought one. Rose acquired considerable kudos from the introduction of her 'very
helpful friend' to number nine, at least from the
main beneficiaries, though Valerie and Mary Ann
were not really part of this circle. Their efforts
to spread the news of Ted's other activities, notably his behaviour with Bee, were variously received. Marjorie, who had seen similar antics in
the college she and Ted both belonged to, found
the stories credible. She was slightly tempted to
relay them to Rose as she had been a little put
out by her exile from Rose's flat during the stay of
her friend Rachel, but found it preferable to enjoy
her friendship and often amusing company when
these were resumed. Ted's help, moreover, was
undeniably useful and a considerable saving on
expensive visits from the professional computer
man. Marjorie was never averse to saving money.
She deemed it unwise to risk alienating Ted and
even defended him when Rose complained about
him, as she often did. The complaints were not,
however, about his attentions to other women,
whom he frequently talked about. Rose not only
met Millie but invited her to view her flat and attended church concerts with her.

They were each taken, in rotation, to dinners in Ted's college. The rota included Bee and even, if less often, Ted's wife. Fortunately she was not accompanying her husband when the college porter remarked with loud joviality on his 'turning up with a different girlfriend every time'. This was overheard by Marjorie, who happened to be dining in the college independently at the same time. She expected Ted to respond with at least some coolness if not an actual comment on the rudeness of such a remark but he seemed rather flattered than otherwise. He was always over-familiar with college servants and in fact seemed more comfortable conversing with them than with other dons. Having been an undergraduate at an older, more prestigious and formal college where the college servants addressed one as 'Madam' or 'Sir', Marjorie was not impressed. She even mentioned it to Rose the next time they were together.

"Oh yes," Rose replied with a sigh. "That porter is quite ghastly. I'm so glad to hear that his behaviour is not the accepted norm. When Rachel was here we were walking past the college one evening and he was standing in the doorway eyeing the passers-by as he usually does and he saw me and shouted out: 'I'd have thought you'd be coming in here to see Ted!' Rachel, of course, said 'How does he know you? Who's Ted?' I was so annoyed. As if it's any of his business."

The conversation continued with a discussion on

the manners and behaviour of servants in general, with each of the women implying that they were accustomed to domestic staff in their childhood. They were both of an age to remember at least some few years before the war, a time when even quite modest middle-class households had at least one servant.

"People knew their place in those days," Rose concluded with a sigh, "and servants were trained to know theirs. Of course they knew everybody's business and talked about it among themselves, but only among themselves, and there was none of this use of their employers' Christian names. Of course I'm afraid Theodore did *not* belong to the servant employing class, that's painfully obvious. Besides, he's younger than I am and probably doesn't remember anything before the war, anyway, and as he's totally unable to read any books other than manuals of instruction he's equally unable to learn about anything outside his own experience."

"You mean he really can't read books — well, what we regard as books?"

"No, I'm afraid not. I tried to get him to read *Brideshead Revisited* but it was totally hopeless. I don't think he ever got past the first chapter and he didn't really take that in."

"How sad. One just has to realise, I suppose, that there are people perfectly intelligent in their own field, very practical and even analytical, who simply cannot read any work of fiction and imagine the places and people in it. Their mind's eye just refuses to see them. Still, never mind, Ted's clearly well able to read cookery books and computer screens, and I suppose that is much more useful."

By chance, Marjorie encountered Ted just as she was going to lunch in the same college the following week. As they passed the lodge the porter hailed them heartily with a jocular greeting and a 'Hullo Ted, got another one with you today!'

"Oh really!" Marjorie cast up her eyes in annoyance.

Ted's only reaction, however, was a particularly fatuous grin and a query to her. "You know Bert, don't you?"

"Yes, unfortunately!"

"Oh, don't you like him?"

"I can't stand over-familiar servants!"

"Well," Ted sounded aggrieved, "Rose loves him; so does Millie."

"*Rose* loves him?"

"Yes; she thinks he's really nice and friendly. She gets on really well with him."

Marjorie digested this in silence. She could not believe Ted was making it up; he had no reason to do so and she doubted whether he had sufficient imagination. It was just possible that he was mistaken and had misread Rose's response to the porter's unseemly jocularity, but then she thought of the Chinese food and Ted's utter unawareness of Rose's dislike of it. She wanted Rose as a friend. She wanted to admire her, in fact to trust her. She had to admit to herself, however, that she felt a disturbing pang of misgiving.

So disturbing, in fact, did Marjorie find Theodore's assurance of Rose's unqualified appreciation of Bert the porter that she determined to ask her about it. No immediate opportunity presented itself, however, as Rose was in fact entertaining Theodore himself that evening. Marjorie hesitated to arrange a specific meeting with Rose as she planned to mention the matter casually in the course of conversation rather than make it sound like an item of importance. Eventually there was a telephone call from Rose inviting — pleading with — Marjorie to come and eat 'yet another Chinese meal'. She accepted with an alacrity not entirely unmixed with trepidation as she was determined to probe the matter of Rose's conflicting opinions, which refused to leave her mind.

The food was up to its usual high standard and the wine generously provided with it made for confidence. "Theodore really is an excellent cook," Marjorie remarked appreciatively. "What a pity you don't like Chinese food."

"Oh, not really; it's a good reason to have you come and eat it for me and I can enjoy your company accordingly."

"But doesn't he ever expect to be here and eat it

with you?"

"I manage to have him cook something else on those occasions, Indian for example — I like that — or Italian. He does some Turkish things too. But we often go out, especially to dinners in his college."

"Oh, of course. I saw him there at lunchtime the other day. I've got dining rights there you know, though I more often go to my undergraduate college. Anyway, we happened to be going in at the same time and that awful porter we were talking about the other day said 'I see you got another one with you today, Ted!' or something to that effect. I expressed some annoyance about it and Ted — Theodore — was quite aggrieved that I didn't like 'Bert'. I told him what I thought about over-familiar college servants and he seemed even more put out and assured me that 'Rose *loved* Bert, and so did Millie.' How can he have thought that? And who's Millie?"

"Oh, I'm sure I've mentioned Millie before. She's that friend of theirs in Headington who lives near them. I've met her a number of times; she often goes to college dinners with him. On special occasions he invites a whole bevy of us, including his wife, and sometimes another couple."

"And does Millie 'love' Bert the porter?"

"Now I think of it she does exchange banter with him. Theodore probably thinks I do too. I doubt whether he notices who says what unless it's directly addressed to him. He certainly wouldn't perceive subtle reactions. But then I find most men are pretty obtuse in that area. Don't you think so?"

"I suppose you're right; some of them even boast about not being very sensitive to atmosphere. I knew an English don who did that, and always put the most unsuitable people together in tutorials."

"I don't really know any English dons apart from you, but I would have expected them to welcome discussion and the exchange of different ideas. Theodore's a scientist, of course, and thinks things are either right or wrong. He doesn't use 'disagreement' as a euphemism for 'row', he actually considers any failure to agree *as* a row. One's expected to like the people he likes and have the same opinions about things as he does. It can be exceedingly tiresome at times. It's really better to have him do useful physical things rather than talk. Women friends are so much more satisfactory to talk to."

The conversation proceeded along mutually pleasing lines and Marjorie finally ascended to her top floor flat feeling completely content with her well spent evening and her friendship with Rose.

CHAPTER 7

Millie was not particularly surprised to receive a telephone call from Rose. They had met more than once at college dinners arranged by Ted.

"Come and have coffee with me," Rose requested. "I know I promised to show you my flat. It's looking reasonably habitable now. Theodore's hung most of the pictures and put up some more bookshelves."

"Oh, thanks ever so much. I'd really like to see it."

Arrangements were made as to date and time and Millie duly arrived at number nine and found her way up the back stairs as directed. Coming from her own immaculate, modern house where nothing was permitted to become worn or shabby or even old-fashioned she was quite shocked at the state of the walls and the stairs with their dingy, worn, faded colours, or resulting lack of colours. The general air was one of uninterested neglect and she wondered how Rose could tolerate such an entrance to her living quarters. She said nothing of this to her hostess, of course. Rose met her at the door of the flat and showed her into it with every appearance of pride. Millie took off her outdoor jacket, a zip up garment of the quilted anorak type, and took the seat offered her on a dark, heavy chair with uncomfortably placed wooden arms. Looking round the room she decided that the rest of the furniture was of a similar age and weight. It was not unlike that in the house occupied by Ted and Emily, but that she was used to and at least it had the air of long occupation and mere lack of incentive to change. It was more understandable than that somebody had deliberately chosen to set it up. Rose was in the kitchen making the coffee so that Millie had time to assume a bland expression and consider what she might say about the flat as clearly some comments on it would be expected. The pictures had been mentioned and at least they could hardly be called uncomfortable. Some of them were in quite light colours even if what they depicted was not immediately identifiable. Millie was surprised to see that they were not all framed and hardly any of them were covered in glass.

Rose came back into the room carrying, with some difficulty, a tray with cups and saucers, a milk jug, a sugar bowl, a plate of biscuits, and what Millie recognised as a coffee maker of the kind she and her friends called a 'cafeteria'. It was not something they used themselves. Their accepted method of making coffee was to boil a mixture of milk and water in a saucepan and, when hot, add it to a mug, or maybe a cup on special occasions, containing a teaspoonful of a good brand of instant coffee granules. Millie had, however, had lunches or dinners in restaurants where coffee was served from a cafetière and so was impressed rather than distressed to see it in Rose's flat.

"So what do you think of my new abode?" Rose enquired.

"Well, Ted's told me a lot about it, of course. It's quite like his place, isn't it? I mean, you must have brought this furniture from where you lived before."

"Oh yes, it's all from The Old Rectory. I'm sorry to say there's a great deal more that I haven't any room for and that's still in store. I think I'll have to take another flat to put it in."

"Couldn't you sell some of it?"

"Oh, I couldn't bear to. I'm thinking of taking the bottom flat in the house next door and putting my other stuff in it and then renting it out. It would be much better than paying for storage."

"That seems like a very good idea. Is it all as big as this furniture? I mean, it must have been very difficult to get it up here."

"Oh, it was quite ghastly. They had to put some of the things through the windows. Ted was here to help and he absolutely *wrecked* his back getting them to place things in the right part of the rooms. I couldn't have managed without him."

"No, he doesn't spare himself, does he. He was

marvellous to me when I had my new suite delivered, even though he never thought I should have got it. He doesn't like new things. He always says 'What's wrong with the old one?' I expect he was happy with your things. Your pictures aren't that old, though, are they?"

"Most of them were done by an artist friend of mine. I nearly always bought one when she had an exhibition. But enough about me and my possessions. How did you enjoy that dinner the other night? What did you think of Theodore's friend Bee?"

"Well, I've met her before, of course, when I've been to Ted's church. She's very, well, flamboyant, isn't she?"

Rose laughed. "That's a clever way of putting it, very charitable. I'm afraid I would have said 'loud and common'. But of course I wouldn't dream of saying so to Theodore."

"No, he does seem to be rather taken with her. People at the church are all talking about it. She's the same age as his daughter, maybe even younger."

Rose laughed again. "People here are talking about it too, though not to me directly. The woman in the flat below mine goes to church especially to report on them. I've heard her talking on the telephone. She doesn't realise how her voice carries when she gets excited. But you probably know her if you go to that church; Mary Ann Evans."

"I don't think I know her."

"Well, she's not very noticeable. Even Theodore doesn't notice her, and he generally notices women. Oh, don't go yet, I must show you over the rest of the flat, not that there's much of it. This is by far the biggest room and I've only got the one bedroom. That's why I really do need something else as well, apart from the furniture problem. I slept on a camp bed when my friend Rachel was here, but it's hardly ideal."

The 'tour' of the premises was soon achieved and Millie was somewhat aghast at the piles of books, the clutter of objects and the ugly furniture of a size even more unsuitable in the smaller rooms. What did surprise her was the dining room with its vastly space-absorbing table. She couldn't resist asking why such a room was considered necessary when it could have been used as a second bedroom.

"Where else could I put the dining-table?" Rose enquired with surprise.

"Couldn't you just put a small one in the sitting-room and get rid — er, sell this big one?"

But Rose had embarked on a history of the dining-table, which was followed by stories associated with other objects. Millie was glad to be spared the necessity of further efforts at appreciation and was not sorry when she finally managed to locate her coat and take her leave.

Ted was delighted that Millie had been to Rose's flat. He never considered the possibility that they could be anything but friends. He was also, of course, anxious for the furnishing and arrangement of the flat to find favour since he had been so instrumental in it. He called round at Millie's especially to hear about it.

"It's a nice flat, isn't it?" he began enthusiastically.

"It looks very much like your place," Millie replied diplomatically.

"How do you mean?"

"Well there's a lot of furniture like yours; bigger if anything. And the bookshelves are the same, of course, since you made them."

"Yes, well, Rose has got a lot of books. There's a lot more furniture, too, only not enough room for it all."

"Hasn't she thought of selling any?"

"No, she doesn't want to do that."

"So I gather. Couldn't you persuade her that if you sell a big house and move into something much smaller you can't take everything with you?"

"She wants to go on the way she's used to. Do you know when she has a meal, even when she's by herself, she always has it in the dining-room with the table set and a proper serviette and everything. She'll just go on and on being the same."

"We can't all do that when we get old."

"We're not going to get old. We're going on and

on."

"How old *is* Rose?"

"Well," Ted appeared to consider, "she says she's older than me but not as old as her friend Audrey, who died a couple of years ago."

"How old was Audrey?"

"I don't know really; about your age. And I'm seventy-four, so I reckon Rose is about seventy-six. Anyway, that's young. There's a lady in Rose's house who's about ninety; you know, the one I told you about who used to be a nun. People do go on and on."

Millie abandoned the attempt to encourage Ted to adopt a more realistic view of things though she was glad the conversation had taken a turn away from Rose's flat as she might have been tempted to say what she really thought of it, which would have offended Ted greatly.

CHAPTER 8

Ted continued to divide his time between Millie, Rose and Bee with rather more of it devoted to Bee than to the others as he saw her every day, except Saturday, at lunchtime and twice on Sundays. She was not, however, equally popular with other members of the church they attended, particularly the female ones. As these formed the bulk of the more active and dedicated of the congregation this was something of a disadvantage. The sacristan, a very academic Lesbian, found her quite repulsively unattractive; the organist, Clarissa Hillman, had always regarded her with disapproval and saw no reason to change her mind; Mary Ann Evans, who had become not only Clarissa's friend but a very regular attender at the church, was entirely of the same opinion. Bee was sufficiently outgoing and insensitive to be unaware of much of the dislike she attracted. She talked so constantly herself that she rarely heard other people say a great deal but even she realised that the woman priest, second in command to the vicar, had it in for her and was cutting her out of services whenever possible. Some of the older and most notably North Oxford members of the congregation returned her effusive salutations with a stoney stare whose overt hostility even so thick-skinned a person as Bee could not fail to recognise. She frequently complained of this treatment to Ted, where she was sure of heartfelt sympathy and even an increase of devotion. Ted was an unfailing champion of distressed damsels. She made a mistake, however, in addressing similar complaints to Clarissa, Mary Ann and Cedric, even though to them it was mainly by way of describing the awfulness of 'those snooty old snobs'.

"Well of course," Mary Ann observed in tones whose acrimony was not immediately apparent, "you'd be much happier in a working-class parish."

Even Bee was too non-plussed at this observation to find an answer and for once was actually reduced to silence. Cedric, who'd barely noticed Mary Ann before, except as an adjunct of Clarissa's, was immediately appreciative.

"Oh my dear" he murmured through a gurgle of his usual giggle, "how terribly true!"

Bee stared at him in disbelief, still said nothing and turned away to find Ted, who was beginning to revert to his former habit of turning up for church only just in time to march in with the rest of the choir and had thus not yet appeared. She would have to wait for commiseration and consolation until after the service.

Ted duly expressed concern and sympathy when made aware of Bee's sufferings, and even felt so strongly about the treatment meted out to her that he called in on Millie rather late that evening to tell her all about it. Bee had indicated that she was too distressed to have him stay with her any longer. She had, in fact, spent the time talking on the telephone to the 'current bloke' instead. Millie was decidedly tired when the scrape of the latch key announced Ted's unexpected arrival. She offered tea, which was refused, and wine, which was accepted. Ted found and opened a bottle of red and they sat over it while Ted talked and Millie stifled yawns and tried to keep her mind on what he was saying. His repeated references to 'poor little Bee' were, however, hard to square with the decidedly solid reality of the person referred to and she found increasing difficulty in producing appropriately sympathetic responses. Words, in fact, did not come at all easily. Her mental picture of the subject grew larger and less and less distinct.

Millie eventually woke up to see that the small hand of the clock on the mantlepiece pointed to four and the large hand to ten and to realise that she was still on the sofa but covered by a rug which Ted must have found in the cupboard under the stairs and thoughtfully thrown over her before departing. She folded it with remarkable neatness and stumbled upstairs to her bedroom murmuring to herself, "well, he really is very kind".

Ted's kindness was, in fact, something Millie often reflected on. Her husband, a good deal older than she was and long dead, had been very much of the old school. He had by no means been an *un*kind man, but one of limited thoughtfulness and the untrammelled opinion that all things domestic were the province of the women in a household and should not be interfered with. Ted, on the other hand, was not only completely at home in a kitchen but very able to anticipate the needs of anybody suffering from ill health of any kind. As Millie tried to go to sleep again after her several hours of dozing on the sofa, she called to mind how Ted had helped her when she had an operation. He had set up an easily movable chair and table; connected a telephone within reach and himself come in regularly to provide meals, attractively served on a tray with matching china, from the very day when she returned from the hospital, where, of course, he had unfailingly visited her at least twice daily. It was true that he had shown considerable interest in almost all the other women on the ward, talking to them as often as he did to her, and had also been likely to telephone at awkward times, even disturbingly late in the evening, but these small things were easily outweighed by the immense amount of help and concern he had shown. Comforted by these reflections and reconciled to the late visit and the entire concentration on the sufferings of 'poor little Bee' Millie drifted off to sleep again.

The following day Rose required 'Theodore' to drive her to her previous place of residence in Hampshire for the purpose of a visit to her dentist and her solicitor. He was, therefore, unable to visit Bee over the lunch hour as he usually did. He'd left a message to this effect on her mobile but had not been able to speak to her before setting out. While he was generally very adept at escaping the company of a woman he was with in order to phone one or more of the women he was not with, and had no qualms whatever about being discovered in this process by his wife and comparatively few about Millie, as long as they couldn't actually hear what he was saying, he was rather more cautious when it came to Rose. He was a little puzzled by this himself if he ever thought about it, though he was by no means given to introspection, nor was he particularly aware of other people's reactions, unless they were made very plain. He had once been seen by his wife, Emily, when they were — unusually — on an outing with another couple, to be talking on his mobile. She had clearly been distressed. 'Who are you phoning, Ted? Who are you phoning? Are you phoning Millie?' she had cried out in tones tinged with an anguish that was not lost on the accompanying couple. As her husband had for once actually been telephoning his department, he responded with what sounded like right-eous indignation and he was far too full of injured innocence to have any comprehension of what Emily was feeling.

Rose talked well. She was interesting to listen to and she never lacked a topic of conversation. Ted would have said he found her easy to talk to, but in fact it was Rose who did ninety per cent of the talking. Between the visit to the solicitor and the visit to the dentist they had a pleasant lunch in an upmarket pub, after which Rose elected to sit outside for coffee. A slight wind began to blow and mar the effect of the sunshine. Rose shivered a lit-tle. Ted immediately took off his jacket and put it round her shoulders; he then sat on the windward side to shield her from the effect of the sudden breeze.

"Oh, you really are *very* kind." Rose was genu-inely appreciative. " 'So loving ....that he might not beteem the winds of heaven Visit her face too roughly' ."

"Pardon?" was Ted's unfortunate response.

Rose's appreciation was a little dented. She was, after all, used to talking to Marjorie, who would not only have known what the words meant but recognised their Shakespearian source. So, she re-flected, would her husband in all probability. But then he would never have deserved to have them quoted about him. What a pity, she mused, that one couldn't take the best bits out of a number of men and put them all together into one really satisfactory one. But aloud she said "Oh it's just a quotation. Here's the coffee. I'll drink it quickly and then we can go back to the car."

Bee had not noticed Ted's absence. She had been taken up with other concerns. He, however, had tried to contact her as soon as he had returned home, quite late, after saying goodnight to Rose. Bee's mobile announced that she was 'not available' so he left another message saying he'd see her the next day. When he went to the church at lunchtime, however, it was locked. He went to the little house by the church hall. There was no answer to the bell. Ted had done his best to acquire a key for himself but had not succeeded. He knocked. He looked in through the windows. There was no sign of life; not much, indeed, even of occupation. He tried Bee's mobile again but she was still 'unavailable'. Eventually he gave up and went, disgruntled, into his college for lunch. The porter greeted him familiarly. "Hullo Ted! Not got a lady-friend with you today! All turned you down, have they?" Even Ted found this salutation faintly annoying; a reputation for numerous 'lady-friends' was one thing, but the suggestion that any of them might have turned him down was quite another, especially coming on top of Bee's sudden uncontactability. He was so preoccupied in pondering her whereabouts that he collected and ate his lunch without so much as pausing to chat up the female staff or even offering his usual pleasantries to the women students of his acquaintance.

Fortunately there was a choir practice at the church that evening. Ted did not invariably attend choir practices. He considered he'd been singing long enough to know the practised works very well. Clarissa Hillman, however, on succeeding the rather laid-back choirmaster before her, had uttered dire threats about non-attenders being suspended from the choir, or even dismissed from it altogether, and after receiving a couple of these Ted had decided to submit and conform. Clarissa had, moreover, altered the way some of the works were sung and Ted had not made himself popular by doing things differently. On this particular evening, however, having still failed to contact Bee after trying all afternoon, he was anxious to find out if anybody else had news of her. The first two choir men he asked showed neither knowledge nor interest. One remarked "Thought you'd have known if anybody did!" and the other merely shrugged. Ted then approached Cedric, who was renowned for his capacity to absorb and retain interesting details about everybody. How he obtained the information was a mystery, but it was almost always accurate.

"Oh, my dear, I would have thought *you* knew!" was Cedric's immediate response to questioning. "She's done a bunk. Simply cleared everything out and gone."

Ted was deeply shocked. "I don't believe it!" was all he could say, though in fact he was distressed rather than genuinely doubtful. "She can't have gone by herself."

"Oh no, she went with that old boy I once took to be her father. You know the one. Not the former husband. He's younger and better looking — in a coarse sort of way."

"You must be talking about the notorious Bee." Clarissa broke in on their conversation. "Yes, the vicar told me about it this afternoon. He seemed rather put out. Not that it matters very much; we don't really need a verger and that cottage ought to be let out for a decent amount of money. But of course she'll be missed by *some* people, won't she, Ted! But come on, this is a choir practice not an old gossips' tea party."

So the practice proceeded with Ted making even more mistakes than usual, which provoked some acid comments from Clarissa and a snide 'excuse' from Cedric. "Oh, the poor pet, you must forgive him; his mind's so obviously on other things!"

Ted had told Rose he'd see her that evening after choir practice so he dutifully went round to number nine, though he would really have preferred to pour his heart out to Millie. He was, however, so full of Bee's unannounced defection that he was unable to talk of anything else. Rose, of course, thanks to Mary Ann Evans and the gossip

which had been audible from her overheard telephone conversations and had filtered through the
house like a leak from a water pipe, knew a great
deal more about Bee than Ted suspected. His own
interest in the departed verger was something he
did not express quite overtly but he was totally
lacking in the finesse to hide it. His main theme
was his shock and distress that she hadn't told him
she was going. Rose responded soothingly by saying "Perhaps it was because she knew you would
try to talk her out of it."

"Well, yes, well I s'pose I would have. I mean, you
know, she was *different!*" Rose smiled a superior
smile and poured Ted another drink.

CHAPTER 9

Ted compensated for the loss of Bee by paying renewed attention to Rose. He was missing the former routine of calling in at the church at lunchtimes and subsequently going out to lunch with female company, but Rose's flat was in the same direction from his department as the church and hardly more distant. It was, therefore, not difficult to avoid the turning to the church and make for 'number nine' instead. Rose made good use of this change of tactics by asking for help of various kinds, particularly with shopping and cooking but also with trips into the country or back to her old haunts in Hampshire. She knew how to make 'Theodore' feel important and necessary, which was balm to his wounded spirit.

After almost a week he managed to contact Bee on her mobile. He had left her numerous messages every day and she had finally found it too annoying to keep her phone switched off in order to avoid him. She was completely unrepentant about her sudden departure and appeared to think it odd that anybody should be unduly surprised.

She had, of course, already walked out on two marriages so it could hardly be considered very important to abandon a job. She also mentioned casually that she and Archie were going to get married as soon as possible and that she'd be inviting everybody to the wedding. "So I'll see you then," she finished. Ted wanted to know more about 'Archie' but the phone had gone off and even he was not quite persistent enough to ring again immediately.

He called in on Millie that evening after leaving Rose rather early because she was going to a concert with Marjorie. Millie was sympathetic. She was also interested in Bee's marriage plans. It would be fun if they all went to the wedding, she considered. She talked about it cheerfully and identified 'Archie' as 'the current bloke' because Bee had often talked to her about him. She did rather wonder what Bee had ever talked to Ted about as he seemed surprisingly ignorant of her background or anything else about her. She concluded that all these things had probably been mentioned, as Bee certainly talked a good deal, but that Ted had simply not listened or not taken them in.

"Is Bee at home with her parents now?" she asked, thinking Ted might at least know that. But as "I don't know" was the reply it was clear that he didn't.

"Perhaps she's staying with her sister?"

"She hasn't got a sister."

"Well, why did she tell me she had?"

"She never told me that." Ted sounded aggrieved.

"I don't suppose you ever asked her."

Ted made an effort to search his mind. He remembered what Bee had said about her marriages and about her operations, particularly the latter as he was better at remembering physical things.

After some reiteration of his grievances over Bee and repetitions of the same conversation, Ted finally made his way home and Millie made herself a cup of tea. It seemed the best pick-me-up after what had been a somewhat demanding and decidedly tiring couple of hours.

The following day Millie was a little surprised to be telephoned by Rose. She immediately supposed the call would have something to do with Bee and Ted's reaction to her unrepentant departure. Rose had occasionally rung before to complain about Ted, usually about his being 'controlling', but this time it was rather different. The complaint was about a linen suit. Rose wanted to buy him one and he refused to have it.

"Oh," Millie managed to repress a giggle before replying, "you want to smarten him up?"

"Well, you must admit it's necessary. *You* buy him shirts, don't you?"

"Only casual summer ones. He had some that were much too tight on him and they did look really bad."

"Quite. And he goes on wearing the same jacket summer and winter till it almost falls off him. He's taking me to see my lawyer in Hampshire and some other people and I can't have him looking like that!"

"Did you try to make him buy the suit?"

"No; I wanted to buy it for him and he said if I did he wouldn't wear it."

"Well, he never does like new things; especially *different* new things. He can't have ever worn a linen suit. Is it a light colour?"

"Yes, a natural creamy beige."

"Don't you think it might make him look a bit sort of big and obvious? And you know if he did have it he'd probably wear it right through the year and all the winter. You know how he is. Perhaps you could persuade him just to buy a new light jacket?"

All Rose managed to reply to Millie's words of wisdom was a wordless exclamation of annoyance. Millie decided to change the subject.

"I suppose you've been hearing all about Bee?" she enquired.

"Who? Oh, that verger woman at his church. No, not really; I hardly knew her. I gather she's gone."

"Yes, very suddenly. She just vanished in a day. Ted seems very upset about it."

"Oh, I can't believe that; he's barely mentioned it

to me and he's been here rather a lot. Of course we've had other things to talk about."

The conversation continued on somewhat uneven lines with each participant firmly, if with superficial politeness, implying that she was more knowledgeable about Ted and his feelings than the other. This was complicated by the fact that neither was willing to suggest that his interest in Bee had superseded his fondness for them. It was an unsatisfactory exchange and Rose caused it to cease abruptly by saying that somebody had rung her doorbell. Millie suspected that this was not true but was not at all sorry to hang up the receiver after a swift goodbye.

It was, of course, not true, and Rose immediately dialled the number of her upstairs friend Marjorie who, she decided, was a much more satisfactory recipient of complaints about Theodore, to which she always responded soothingly and with compliments as to his kindness and with no pretensions as to competition. Marjorie willingly descended the stairs to Rose's flat and they spent a garrulously happy evening together.

As it was a Saturday Ted spent the evening cooking at home. His wife, Emily, busied herself with the rearranging of the contents of two large bookshelves on the upstairs landing. She knew somebody who put all their books into alphabetical order of authors, but as that would involve books in other parts of the house it was clearly too daunting a task, so she merely placed the works of the same authors together. This was not very time consuming so she progressed to the bathroom, and made an effort to clean it. There was a patch on the floor where the linoleum had completely worn away because the door stuck and refused to close properly. By the window there was a hole in the wall, which let in blasts of cold air whatever the outside temperature. Emily did keep the room surprisingly clean, but it was not a very rewarding task. Ted could have rectified the worst of these signs of neglect without a very significant expenditure of effort, but the vast amount of time and energy he spent helping Millie and Rose, especially Rose, not to mention Bee before her disappearance, left little of either to be devoted to improvements at home. Emily had occasionally been heard to murmur, when any mention was made of her husband's usefulness in services to others, 'that there was plenty to do at home', but Ted appeared deaf to these murmurs and the only thing he did at home was to cook. Of course the cooking was happily interspersed by visits to the garden, where he smoked a cigarette and drank gin and tonic and telephoned various numbers on his mobile. He was a little piqued to find that both Millie's and Rose's landlines gave the engaged signal and wondered whether they might be speaking to each other. In fact he failed to contact Rose until very late that night as she simply allowed her phone to go on ringing while she was talking to Marjorie. Bee's phone was switched off as usual, but he left her a number of messages.

On the following day, Sunday, Mary Ann Evans went to church early as usual and was immediately apprised by Clarissa of Bee's sudden departure.

"Now that's very interesting because we've been noticing that Theodore has been in number nine at lunchtimes again. Valerie's none too pleased because of course he's using her car space. Rose must be back in position as *la favorita*."

"That's hardly surprising," Clarissa responded, "but rather a pity in some ways; it may be more amusing for the occupants of your house but it was quite a source of excitement here. Of course people were *most* disapproving and desperately sorry for Emily, but that didn't stop anybody being agog with animated interest."

Cedric sashayed up to Clarissa's side. "Now, darling, I simply can't imagine *what* you're talking about, can I? Poor dear deserted Ted *can't* be consoling himself already! And of course *nobody's* disappointed at the absence of anybody to be scandalised about, are they?"

"Really, Cedric, you're so naughty!"

"Nonsense, darling, it's exactly what you were

saying yourself - in very slightly different words. Never mind. I gather we're *all* going to be invited to the wedding. Then at least we'll have something to talk about for a week or two after. Oh, but here's the grieving lover; I'll go into the vestry in case he thinks we're talking about him."

Cedric floated into the vestry singing softly "Sing all a green willow/ Willow, willow willow/ Sing all a green willow /My garland shall be." Which might well have caused Ted to realise that Cedric had been talking about him had he been at all aware that wearing willow garlands was the sad token of those disappointed in love. Perhaps it was fortunate that the symbolism escaped him entirely as did any knowledge of literary precedents. He merely shuffled himself into his cassock and surplice.

Clarissa advanced on the organ and Mary Ann took up her usual place halfway down the nave. By the time the processing choir reached her they were singing "Redeem thy mis-spent time that's past/ And live each day as if thy last". Mary Ann glanced at Ted as he passed the end of her pew and wondered if he ever thought about the meaning of what he was singing. In fact he knew the hymn so well that he was singing the words quite mechanically.

Moreover, he would have been very surprised and considerably offended and hurt had he supposed that anybody might consider any of his time mis-spent.

After the service Clarissa and Mary Ann went to the Royal Oak for a drink, where they agreed that the absence of Bee rendered the atmosphere in the church rather flat.

"Well at least you can go back to number nine and see whether Ted's car's there and how long it stays," was Clarissa's consolation to Mary Ann.

"I expect it will be there; Rose seems to be back in position as *la favorita!* We do wonder how she felt about the relegation. But she's hardly likely to let us know."

CHAPTER 10

Ted continued to be much in evidence at number nine. In addition to helping Rose with anything and everything and ferrying her round the country or the town as the fancy took her, albeit without wearing a linen suit or any other garment different from his usual garb, he helped Benedicta with her shopping, aided and guided Marjorie with the mysteries of her computer, practically performed the functions of a general factotum to the whole household with undemanding kindness. Even Mary Ann and Valerie had grudgingly to admit that he was useful. They were inclined to suspect, almost to hope, that he had an ulterior motive, but had so far been unable to detect one.

Mary Ann continued to attend church services and further her friendship with Clarissa, diligently reporting on Ted's activities at number nine; but interest in these was no longer fuelled by any strong reason for criticism of his behaviour in or around the church, apart from late appearances and the occasional failure to attend choir practices and lack of attention to his wife. Mercifully, however, this rather stale situation was invaded by the arrival of an invitation from Bee to attend her wedding in Chelmsford Cathedral. The adult members of the choir and all the church's core congregation were included. This was not a very vast number but might run to a bus load. They were all bidden to the service and to drinks and nibbles in the cathedral. Ted was cock-a-hoop because he and Emily, and for some reason Millie, had also been included in the reception proper, to take place in a hotel in Dunmow.

Given the disapproval generally vented on or over Bee while she was verger of the church, it was perhaps surprising that quite a number of people showed a willingness, in fact a barely hidden eagerness, to attend her wedding. It appeared that nobody had ever been to Chelmsford and few had been aware that it contained a cathedral; considerable interest was expressed in seeing the place and enjoying the trip as a day out, facilitated by being taken there and brought back in a bus. Apart from some of the younger choir men, the majority of members of the congregation belonged to the age group which regarded independent travel as something not to be undertaken lightly, but rejoiced in excursions organised by others. Many of them were frequently to be seen on outings run by and for Friends of the Ashmolean and similar societies. A trip to a previously undiscovered cathedral, with drinks and nibbles thrown in, not to mention a wedding to discuss, was by no means an unattractive prospect.

Mary Ann Evans was a little surprised at Clarissa's interest in attending the wedding. She was not of the age group to be unwilling to drive about the country on her own and she had certainly not been a fan of Bee's. Cedric, however, was rather more perceptive. He came into their conversation with "Of *course* Clarissa wants to go and see the show! We *all* do. Things have been so *desperately* dull lately. There's been absolutely *nothing* to talk about except the feud between the curate and the sacristan, and even that's hardly been so openly visible as to excite general attention. This wedding will provide opportunities for acid comments for weeks to come. I wouldn't miss it for *anything!* Besides, I wonder if they'll have the Chelmsford cathedral choir. Heaven *knows* what sort of music they'll choose. Do you think they might have *The Bees' Wedding* during the signing of the register? Now that *would* be fun!"

"It'd certainly be more appropriate than most of the things one hears at weddings like *Oh for the Wings of a Dove* or *Panis Angelicus* — when there isn't even any communion. And it would certainly be lively; though I don't know how many of the congregation would appreciate the joke. Or the music, come to that," Clarissa spoke feelingly. "But surely," she continued, "it won't be the full works, I mean an actual marriage service. She's been married twice before and I can't believe it's his first marriage either."

"Oh no, it isn't. He's got a grown up family but they won't have anything to do with him."

"Really, Cedric, how do you know these things?" Clarissa was genuinely impressed.

"Oh, you know, darling, grapevine. But it wouldn't be the first time I've seen a full works church wedding for somebody with an ex still living."

"No, really?" Mary Ann had, until recently, been rather out of date as regards church practices. "An *Anglican* church wedding?"

"Oh, well, yes, it does happen, though not so often now people can get married almost anywhere — like on the top of a mountain or on a train or at The Eden Project. I heard of a couple of quite old people getting married there, and apparently the guests couldn't hear a thing because of a waterfall somewhere near and it was awfully hot and one of the older women fainted. But I suppose they were pretending to be in the Garden of Eden." Clarissa was rather dismissive of the whole business.

"How terribly funny," said Cedric, "and hardly propitious! Did they all try to sing *The voice that breathed o'er Eden?* That used to be a great favourite."

"I had that at my wedding," Mary Ann remembered suddenly. "My mother insisted on it. It certainly wasn't very propitious, either."

As the wedding reception was to be in a sizeable hotel in the High Street of Great Dunmow, Ted and Emily and Millie decided to stay there for the night. They were all, in different ways, quite excited at the prospect. Millie, despite her age, was a seasoned and intrepid traveller, who always enjoyed an excursion and was never averse to 'going posh', as she put it. She was also of the opinion that there was no entertainment like a good wedding. Emily was delighted because for her to travel anywhere was a rare treat, though she did occasionally go on day trips with her daughter. To go and stay in a hotel with Ted was an even rarer treat. She was not particularly phased by the fact that Millie would be there too, but at least it meant that Ted would not be disappearing to ring her up all the time. Of course he'd probably ring Rose, but she was likely to keep herself busy with other people while he was away and give him short shrift if she answered at all. Ted himself was most delighted that he had received such a special invitation. It was a mark of favour from Bee that he'd hardly have dared hope for. Besides, he really did want to see her again. He left messages on her mobile to that effect every day. Bee reflected that it was just as well she'd invited him or he'd be homing in on the reception with his numerous phone calls!

Such was Ted's enthusiasm for the projected wedding attendance that he was unable to suppress it even when talking to Rose, who knew Bee very slightly and could hardly have been expected to exhibit great interest. She bore Ted's somewhat lengthy treatment of the subject with great equanimity, however, as she simultaneously made mental plans to have her friend Rachel to stay while he was away. She smiled happily as she envisaged the relief afforded by such different company, a smile which conveyed to Ted nothing but appreciation of his presence and conversation.

The great day finally arrived. Ted, Emily and Millie set off to cover the miles to Great Dunmow in Ted's very old and not very large or comfortable car and the other members of the Oxford contingent set off a little later in a large and relatively comfortable bus to cover a similar distance to Chelmsford, where they were all to have lunch, either purchased in a restaurant by the extravagant or brought in tupperware by the frugal, before attending Bee's wedding. Clarissa and Mary Ann sat together with Cedric in a neighbouring seat on the other side of the bus. They were betting on the most likely hymns in the service.

"Well," said Clarissa, "judging from the numerous weddings where I've played the organ I'd expect *Dear Lord and Father of mankind / Forgive our foolish ways etc etc.*"

"That would certainly be appropriate," Mary Ann

commented, "especially nowadays, when they all live together before they're married."

"Some of it, yes," Cedric agreed, "like *In purer lives Thy service find,* but what about later on where it says *Let sense be dumb, let flesh retire*, now that can only be considered *totally* inappropriate at a wedding. How disastrous if *either* of them thinks of it that night! Well, particularly if only *one* of them does."

Clarissa laughed. "I've often thought of that. But it probably doesn't matter so much now when they've been at it for years."

"You have a point there, darling, but you know the marriage has to be *consummated* to be *valid.*" Cedric knew his theology.

"That's true enough," Clarissa admitted, "but not necessarily on the wedding night. And at least these days we're spared the sort of ghastly suggestive speeches by the best man that used to be practically standard."

"I don't suppose there'll be anything of that kind this time," Mary Ann was determined not to be left out of the conversation, "when the bride's already been married twice before!"

"We won't be hearing any speeches anyway as we're not going to the main reception. I can't imagine they'll have anybody trying to speechify with the drinks in the cathedral after the service. We'll have to ask Ted and Emily about the rest of it. They seem to be the only people invited to the dinner." Clarissa, like the choir members, had been treated to Ted's frequent mention of this fact, which had by no means diminished his satisfaction in being thus singled out.

Lunches of various kinds having been consumed, the bus load from Oxford were shown into the cathedral by a sidesman or similar official in a distinctive russet coloured gown. The central part of the building was already fairly full. Clarissa, Cedric and Mary Ann whispered their surprise at the size of the congregation and thumbed through the Order of Service booklets with which they had been presented.

"Good heavens, it's a whole, full service!" Mary Ann mouthed inaudibly. "How can they have that when both the bride and groom have exes still alive?"

"Well, I hadn't expected that, I must admit," Clarissa spoke more audibly, "but I believe he's something to do with the cathedral — and maybe they know somebody!"

"It really is rather appalling the way anything goes these days, especially if you know the right people." Cedric was dismissive.

"You'd have thought Prince Charles knew the right people," Mary Ann objected, "and all he was allowed was a registry office wedding and a church blessing."

"Poor fellow; I fear he knew exactly the *wrong* people," said Cedric, "especially his mother. After all, she is supposed to be head of the Anglican Church."

"I suppose he was lucky to be allowed to marry Camilla at all, when you think what things used to be like. I remember when there was that Peter Townsend business with Princess Margaret."

"Oh really, darling, surely you can't remember that!" Cedric was less genuinely surprised than he was happy to draw attention to Mary Ann's advanced years.

"Well," Mary Ann replied somewhat defensively, "I was a child at school, of course. I remember our headmistress being very scathing about it. She said 'If the Archbishop of Canterbury allows that little trollop of a Princess Margaret to marry Peter Townsend I'll go over to Rome!' But as he didn't she stayed a High Anglican."

Mary Ann's voice had risen to an almost normal level and an occupant of the pew in front of theirs turned round to glare at her. Fortunately the organ began to sound and conversation ceased.

The music switched from Bach to *Here comes the bride* ("Well *really*!" was the audible comment from Clarissa) and everybody stood up and turned round to stare at the west end as the bride approached. She was clad in a long white dress of the fashionable style with bare flesh rising from the barely covered bosom. A large wreath of white flowers stood out from her head. As she proceeded down the aisle on the arm of, presumably, her father, a plump and rather bald man not much taller than she was, the train of her dress rustled along the floor for a couple of yards. It was undeniably impressive.

The service was indeed 'the full works' and the hymns were disappointingly innocuous: *Now thank we all our God* and *Praise to the holiest in the height.* Even Cedric could only point out that the *countless gifts of love* referred to in the first were rather too clearly appropriate for this bride, and that if marriages were made in heaven the *loving wisdom* of the Lord, so highly praised in the second, had been somewhat lacking on two previous occasions. Nevertheless the total was highly satisfactory and, as Cedric had predicted, provided a wealth of material for acidic criticism for weeks, if not years to come. The congregation from Oxford loaded themselves into their coach, after the fortification provided by crisps, nuts and raisins and other packeted means of sustenance washed down by a glass (two for the swift and devious or very fortunate) of sparkling white wine, with a general sense of satisfaction.

CHAPTER 11

Rose filled in the time of Ted's absence very happily with her visit from Rachel, mainly in relief from Ted's usually over-frequent presence and in complaining about this to her friend. She was even less disturbed than usual by his telephone calls as he was with his wife a good deal of the time and had less opportunity to indulge in them. It was, in fact, a slightly happier time than usual all round, although of short duration. Rachel went home, Ted returned and visited number nine with great promptitude and lengthy descriptions of what was, to him, the wedding of the year. Rose listened with pleasantly simulated interest, examined the Order of Service without adverse comment, and came up with a large shopping list, which of course she needed Ted's help to purchase from a relatively distant supermarket. They talked of the wedding all the way there, though Ted was unable to come up with any really interesting details, such as what the bride was wearing or whether any members of the bridegroom's family were to be seen. Nevertheless it passed the time and the necessary shopping was stowed into the car and brought back to the flat without any physical effort on Rose's part.

More interest was in fact to be gleaned from Mary Ann's account of the occasion. None of the other inhabitants of number nine had ever encountered the notorious Bee, but her role as a rival to Rose had rendered her worthy of notice, even at secondhand, and news of her dress — 'totally unsuitable for a woman who'd been married before, let alone *twice* before' — and the paucity of the drinks and nibbles supplied after the service — which was just as unsuitable as the dress' — spread round the house with satisfying speed. Benedicta was heard to murmur charitably that at least Bee was married and not merely living with the chap and that anything went with the Anglicans, anyway. Valerie remarked that second wives generally had a better time than first ones and maybe the same could be said for husbands. Marjorie said 'Thridde time throw best', but she was quoting a medieval text, which could hardly be considered relevant to the present situation. Mary Ann wondered aloud how long it would be before Bee was boasting about having *three* ex-husbands. Rose managed to appear in agreement with every opinion expressed, without actually expressing anything herself.

On the following Saturday morning Millie was awakened unusually early by a telephone call from Ted. "I probably won't be in today," he said in tones breathless with anxiety. "I'm in the hospital where I've just been with Rose. She was taken in an ambulance. She rang me to say she had a terrible pain in her stomach. The ambulance arrived at her place at the same time as I did. I helped them get her into it. Well, as much as they'd let me. The doctors are with her now."

"That sounds like appendicitis," was Millie's sensible observation.

"No, she's had her appendix out; years ago. It can't be that."

"But it's not life threatening." Millie had worked as a doctor's receptionist and was not greatly given to alarm taking.

"They don't know!" Ted, who *was* greatly given to alarm taking, sounded as if he was barely holding back the tears. Millie replied soothingly and told him not to worry and to let her know if she could do anything to help; put down the receiver and thought little more about it.

She merely reflected that Emily was unlikely to have a meal cooked for her that evening and that she herself could enjoy doing exactly as she wanted to do and watch her favourite television programmes without the interruption of frequent telephone calls as Ted would doubtless go back to the hospital for the evening visiting hours.

The inhabitants of number nine were all equally agog and distressed at Rose's sudden and unforeseen departure in an ambulance. She had shown no unusual sign of illness the day before. Inquiries as to her welfare had elicited only vague answers from the hospital and it was generally agreed that weekends were not the best times for admissions.

"Or for treatments or anything else!" Marjorie commented grimly. Frequently an in-patient herself she could speak from experience. "Ted went with her, of course, so perhaps he'll let us know."

Mary Ann and Benedicta, to whom this was addressed as they sat in Mary Ann's flat over a cup of tea, asked if Ted had Marjorie's telephone number.

"He can surely find it out; it's in the telephone book. I've got his Department one in the University telephone book, but I don't suppose that's any good. His home one should be easy to find though; I'll ring him there if we don't hear soon."

"Do it from here if you like; I'll find the number." Mary Ann was more generous with the use of her telephone than Marjorie was inclined to be and the offer was gratefully received.

"Oh, hullo Emily; Marjorie Reed here. You know, we've often met in college. I'm just ringing to ask if Ted has any news about Rose. We can't get much sense out of the hospital. ...... What? Not at all? Oh I see. Well if you could just mention that I rang.....my number's in the book. Yes, thank you so much. Goodbye." She put down the receiver and turned to the others. "Well really! He hasn't been home at all and hasn't even rung his wife. And he was here when the ambulance arrived at half past seven this morning. And now it's almost five o'clock."

"He can't have been in the hospital all that time, surely!" Mary Ann was incredulous. "But presumably his wife's used to not knowing where he is. I never knew where my husband was all day. I don't think I cared a lot. Probably his wife doesn't either."

"I can't imagine that she does or she wouldn't be able to put up with him." Marjorie spoke with some authority. "He often behaves atrociously with other women in college and usually his wife just sits there smiling, or talks to people and takes no notice. She and Ted almost always arrive and leave separately."

There was no telephone call from Ted to Marjorie or any of the inhabitants of number nine that day, but Millie was less able to enjoy a peaceful, call-free evening than she had expected. Her phone rang at about eight o'clock and Ted's tired voice addressed her as usual with "Hullo love, it's me."

"Oh Ted, where are you?"

"At the hospital, of course."

Have you been there all day?"

"Yes, I have."

"How is Rose?"

There was a pause and what sounded like a sob.

Ted?" Millie repeated.

There was another sob and then a muffled "Pretty

100

bad. They've given her antibiotics but not done much else."

"You don't sound very well yourself. Have you had anything to eat?"

"No. I don't want anything."

"You should keep your strength up; you won't be much use if you get ill yourself. Why don't you go home now and have something. Come and have a drink here on the way if you like."

"No. I'm giving up drinking and smoking."

"Why?"

"Maybe if I do that God will let her live."

"Now really, Ted; they don't even know what's wrong yet. Or how bad it is or anything. I mean, praying's fine, but aren't you going over the top?"

"It looks bad."

"Oh, now, you're over-reacting. And you can't be doing Rose any good sitting there all full of distress and alarm. I'm surprised the hospital staff haven't told you to go away."

"They have actually. That's why I'm outside the ward ringing up. But I'm going back."

Millie gave up the unequal struggle and decided to let the ward staff deal with the situation. She knew how stubborn Ted could be, so she sighed resignedly and said goodbye and hoped for better news the next day.

The next day, however, the news was much the same and so was Ted's demeanour. He went to the hospital shortly after eight a.m., without even taking the usual cup of tea up to Emily, as she rarely wanted one before nine. He himself had nothing but a drink of water. Rose was asleep when he went into the ward; she was kept fairly heavily doped on painkillers, though these were not always a hundred per cent effective. Ted drew up a chair by the bedside and tenderly took Rose's hand. She stirred, opened her eyes, saw him and closed her eyes again. She made a feeble attempt to withdraw her hand but so feeble that Ted barely noticed it. He was reading the hospital tag on her wrist. It gave her name as Rose and her age as — Ted gave a gasp and a disgusted exclamation, they'd obviously got it wrong — eighty-seven! She'd told him she was seventy-six! Well, he reflected, as he tried to remember the occasion; not exactly *told* him. He'd suggested seventy-six and she hadn't denied it. His initial determination to complain to the hospital staff about their 'mistake' gave way to doubt. After all, even if it was a mistake it didn't really matter; what did matter was the diagnosis and treatment, neither of which seemed to be forthcoming. Seeing that Rose was apparently asleep Ted slid his hand out of hers and went to the nurses' station. Here he demanded to know when the doctor would be coming, and what was going to be done. The rather junior nurse in occupation replied politely that she would inquire from somebody more senior and let him know.

"Well, I hope that won't take too long. She came in yesterday morning and nothing was done except to give her painkillers and antibiotics. Anybody could have done that. I don't care if it's the weekend; people don't only get ill on weekdays. Hospitals should be able to deal with emergencies at all times."

"I'm sure you'll be able to see the doctors when they come in. They'll be able to tell you."

A more senior nurse passing the station saw that the junior was having something of a struggle to placate an apparently anxious relative and came to intervene. She was treated to the same, if slightly heightened, tirade from Ted and gave the same answer but in sterner and less placatory tones. She also advised him to leave the ward for a time and come back later, but that he refused to do. He returned to the bedside, was with difficulty persuaded to have a cup of tea, mainly by Rose, who woke up sufficiently to speak to him. He reiterated his complaints about her lack of treatment, which was hardly consoling. Rose replied that after all he had no real authority to demand any explanations from the doctors when they came to the ward.

"Can't I say I'm your next of kin? Who have you put as next of kin? It ought to be me."

"Oh, of course, but they haven't asked about that. I don't think it's essential. I'll deal with it when they ask. Don't worry about it now. Can you telephone Marjorie some time and say I'd like to see her. And Benedicta, too. I can tell you the numbers."

Ted duly entered the numbers on his mobile phone then went out of the ward to do the telephoning. There was no answer from Benedicta but Marjorie was at home and pleased to hear from him, thinking he was responding to her message and request to ring her. As he was quite blank about this, however, it transpired that he had had so little contact with Emily that he had not in fact received it, but that he was ringing her at Rose's request. Marjorie was delighted at this, if less delighted to hear of the supposed failings of the hospital, though she took Ted's obvious distress as an indication of his feelings rather than the actual facts. She had intended to visit that afternoon anyway, and Ted's call saved her the trouble and expense of ringing the hospital herself.

When the doctor, accompanied by a couple of acolytes, finally came round Ted endeavoured to treat him to the same barrage of complaints with which he had already treated the nurses. The doctor tried to give him short shrift with a very brief and succinct series of reasons for the course of treatment pursued so far. Seeing, however, that this not entirely unknowledgeable layman was bent on continuing to be aggressively argumentative he said he'd see him later in the ward waiting room if he wished to discuss the case further. Ted calmed a little and agreed to this with something like gratitude. He had, of course, to wait until the whole ward round was finished. He filled in the time by reassuring Rose that he would persuade the medical team to do all the right things for her. She smiled wearily and advised him to go and wait in the proper place so that he would be sure not to miss his consultation with the doctor. Eventually, and without the support of his acolytes, the doctor came to speak to Ted. He began authoritatively: "Now Mr Er..."

"*Dr* if you don't mind," Ted corrected immediately.

"Oh, I'm sorry. I didn't realise you were a medical man." The doctor was considerably younger than Ted and feared he was dealing with a retired physician with fixed, archaic and of course erroneous views.

"I'm not; I'm a physicist. A D.Phil. This university."

"Ah; I see." Relief was apparent. "Now about your partner's condition."

Ted opened his mouth to correct the doctor again and deny such a relationship but then thought better of it and decided to let it pass. Instead he said "It's the treatment, or lack of it, that I'm concerned about."

"Well, you must realise that the problem is due to peritonitis for which the standard treatment is antibiotics."

"She's not responding to the antibiotics. Can't you operate to find out why?" Ted enquired somewhat aggressively.

"Now that would be very much a last resort in somebody of such an age."

"She doesn't seem that old. She could pass for ten or twelve years younger." Ted omitted to say that Rose had in fact been doing so very successfully.

"That may be so, especially to a biased observer, but facts are facts, and she is in *fact* nearer ninety than eighty and not of a very suitable age for an exploratory operation. And you should also realise that your complaining about her treatment is very disturbing for her. You'd do much better for her peace of mind if you could assure her that everything is being done for the best. Surely you can see that."

Ted could at least see that there was no point in arguing, however much he himself believed in Rose's inherent youthfulness. He managed to murmur some not very gracious thanks for the consultant's time and take himself back to the ward to sit with Rose. It was lunchtime (or dinner time, as most of the ward's inhabitants called it); Rose was ineligible for solid food and being fed by means of drips and tubes. Ted was with some difficulty persuaded to have a cup of tea.

He was still sitting by Rose's bed when Marjorie came to visit her that afternoon. As he insisted on staying there conversation was somewhat inhibited even though Rose was quite well awake. Marjorie suggested that he go and ring Benedicta, but he responded with "Won't you be able to see her and tell her how Rose is?" Marjorie could only reply that she would, of course, and conversation languished again. Fortunately, however, the idea of a telephone call reminded Ted that it was rather a long time since he'd rung Millie, so he said he'd do that while Marjorie was there "to look after Rose." In his absence Rose managed to make it clear to her housemate that she was finding Ted's continual presence somewhat wearing and his attitude to the hospital staff by no means helpful. She had, however, managed to contact her friend Rachel, who would be coming from Hampshire and staying in her flat so that she could come to the hospital each day, hopefully making Ted's attendance less persistent. She could say no more as Ted returned to the ward and announced that Millie sent her love. Marjorie made some rather pointed remarks about 'not overstaying her welcome' and 'knowing from experience that visitors could be very tiring when one was in hospital' — all of which were entirely lost on Ted — and took her leave.

Back at number nine Marjorie felt the lack of her friend Rose and the need to talk about the whole situation so she telephoned Mary Ann and suggested they have a cup of tea together. As she had hoped Mary Ann responded with an invitation to come and join her as she'd just put the kettle on and put some tea in the pot.

"Well, and how was Rose looking? She's clearly allowed visitors, and I suppose Ted — Theodore — was there as he wasn't in church and his wife Emily came up to Clarissa (the organist, you know) saying he wouldn't be singing in the choir because a friend of his was ill in hospital. She seemed to think that was enough to explain his absence."

Marjorie responded to the various points contained in Mary Ann's voluble greeting as she gratefully sipped her very good tea from Fortnum and Mason. "Well really, Theodore was looking nearly as bad as Rose. Apparently he's hardly left her bedside and won't even eat anything. She couldn't say much to me as he was there almost all the time, but he did go out briefly and ring Millie. Do you know Millie?"

"Oh yes. He's brought her to church occasionally. Apparently she lives near them and he takes her meals and so on. Well, not just now, of course. He can't be at home to cook as usual."

"Nor for anything else, apparently. How did his wife seem? I don't suppose she's surprised." Marjorie spoke from experience.

"Not at all. She spoke as if it was quite normal and to be expected." "Yes, I'm afraid it is, from him."

"Well at least she knows where he is," Mary Ann made a face. "More than I did with my wretch."

"So you don't think she should divorce him? A lot of people are surprised she hasn't."

"Hmm," Mary Ann considered reflectively, "that does rather depend on the settlements. But she doesn't seem to be the type to spend much. Some of the church people say she should have been a nun; she lives as if she's taken a vow of poverty: she'll never take a taxi, walks or buses everywhere, regards butter as a treat only to be had at Christmas and Easter. She probably thinks of him as a sort of penance to be put up with for the good of her soul."

"That's not unlikely. And he rarely concentrates on just one other woman. Or not for long, anyway. He's not at all likely to divorce Emily and go off with any of them. The older ones are older than he is and glad of his help and attention but probably don't want to give up their freedom. They've got the sense and experience to realise they're not his only interest, too. Seeing how he treats his wife should put any but the most starry-eyed off marrying him. And the younger ones go off with somebody else. I've seen that happen more than once."

Mary Ann gave a giggle. "I can't imagine Ted inspiring anybody to go 'starry-eyed'! Not even if he's called 'Theodore'!"

They both laughed. There was a knock at the door. "Now who?" said Mary Ann and, "come in!" in almost the same breath. It was Benedicta.

"I came to see if you had any news about Rose, but it can't be too bad as you're both laughing. Well, you were when I knocked."

Marjorie and Mary Ann both felt very slightly ashamed. Benedicta never preached and never reproached anybody directly if they made snide comments or gave vent to uncharitable remarks, but she never did anything of the sort herself and was quite unconsciously the kind of person who brings out the best in everybody else, though she had a sane, unsentimental view of human nature and was rarely taken in by superficial charm or insincerity.

"Oh, Benedicta, have a cup of tea," said Mary Ann.

"Oh, Benedicta," said Marjorie, almost simultaneously, "I'm so glad you're here. Rose says she'd love to see you. She wanted Theodore to ring you but he, er - I said I'd be seeing you anyway. Rose is very feeble, I'd say, but of course she's all drips and drugs and so on and one could hardly expect anything else. But she does appreciate visits. I'll take you up there in the car tomorrow if you like. Then you can judge for yourself."

So the question of the cause of laughter never arose.

CHAPTER 12

Rose's friend Rachel duly arrived and went to the hospital. There, of course, she encountered Ted, greatly to their mutual dissatisfaction. Despite all hints to allow the women to speak to each other in private, Ted maintained his position by the bedside. There was no apparent improvement in Rose's condition though she was clearly cheered to see her friend. She was, however, overtaken by pain rather worse than usual and Ted, alarmed, went to find a nurse and make his usual demands for tests, treatment and doctors. Weakened himself by lack of food and sleep, and doubtless rendered unhappy by the presence of Rachel, he began to weep copiously. The nurse remonstrated "Now, now, you're not going to do the patient any good carrying on like this. Go and have a cup of tea and something to eat and don't come back till you've calmed down."

Ted, however, blew his nose with several fog-horn blasts and went back to Rose's room. He was still crying when a senior nurse came in and gave Rose an injection. Rose looked helplessly from Ted to Rachel and Rachel turned on Ted and told him roundly to go away.

"Can't you see you're upsetting Rose? Go away and pull yourself together. It's very tactless of you to be here all the time; tactless and intrusive."

Ted blew his nose again and then bent over Rose. "Do you want me to go?" he asked her.

"I want you to go and have something to eat; please go now," Rose replied feebly. "I want to try and sleep, anyway."

"Then Rachel should go too." Ted was anxious to give no ground.

"I'm not going till you've gone," Rachel was clearly determined to see him leave.

Rose looked at him beseechingly "Please Theodore!" she murmured.

Ted finally left the room, wiping his eyes and choking with sobs. As he passed the nurses' station he blew his nose with another fog-horn blast. "Poor chap," the junior nurse said sympathetically. "Hmm," the senior nurse responded, "I somehow can't empathise with a person who makes that sort of noise when he blows his nose. It does kind of take away from the pathos!"

Ted did leave the ward but he didn't leave the hospital. He went round the car park until he spotted Rachel's car, then managed to move his own to a position from which he could see when Rachel drove away. After some forty minutes she did so and he very promptly went back to the ward again. Rose was in fact asleep, not merely pretending to be, and he took up his usual position by the bedside. He was there when Marjorie came to visit in the early afternoon. Rose was awake by then though frequently closing her eyes and not very willing to speak; she brightened a little when Marjorie appeared and managed to say how nice it was to see her. Ted, glad to see Marjorie rather than Rachel, rose to allow her to sit in his chair and did actually go out of the room after a couple of minutes.

"Oh, Marjorie," Rose addressed her urgently, "Theodore's here almost *all* the time and he gets so upset and weeps and sobs and speaks angrily to the nurses. It's so embarrassing: they all think he's my lover and of course you know he isn't. It's terrible. Somebody must help me; I simply can't cope with it. I tried to tell Rachel but she wanted me to stop upsetting myself, though she did say she'd deal with it and then I went to sleep while she was here, and Theodore's so hostile to her. I don't know if they'll take any notice of her. Oh dear it is distressing."

Marjorie promised to speak to the nurses on her way out and enquire what could be done. She did her best to comfort Rose and told her of the good wishes of all at number nine and Benedicta's intention to visit. They were speaking of this when Ted reappeared. He seemed a little less unhappy but showed his displeasure in his face when Rose asked whether Marjorie had met Rachel yet. The answer was in the negative as of course Rachel had already spent a good deal of time in the hospital. "I think you'll find she's quite a private person," Rose warned.

Somewhat inhibited by Ted's presence Marjorie stayed only a short time. She stopped at the nurses' station on her way out and fortunately found the most senior nurse there. "Mrs Thorneycroft has asked me to speak to you," she began, "she's rather upset."

"Oh?" the nurse feared the kind of complaint she had already endured from Ted. "Who? Oh yes, Rose. We're doing all we can for her."

"Yes indeed; it's not about her treatment, it's about her frequent male visitor. She wants it known that he's not her - er - partner and that she finds his behaviour distressing. Can anything be done about it?"

"Well, we can hardly do anything about his behaviour, but his visits could be stopped if the patient requested this herself. It's only done in fairly extreme cases, but he could be banned from the ward. We'd have to consult senior people to put it in force."

"I think she finds it difficult to speak to anybody as he's here almost all the time. I don't suppose the night staff could deal with it."

"Well, leave it with me and I'll try to speak to her."

Marjorie left the ward feeling she'd done her best; the nurse became occupied with other patients whose conditions demanded much more urgent and immediate attention and finally went off duty while Ted was still keeping his watch by Rose's bedside.

He was still there when Rachel returned some time later. Rose was asleep so they had reason not to speak to each other, which was probably just as well. It was something of a war of attrition, a competition to see who had the longer staying power. Rachel had had the good sense to bring a book to read. It saved her from the necessity of looking at Ted or studiously avoiding looking at him and also rendered her relatively impervious to his attitude of hostility.

It was surprising that Ted was able to endure such long periods of inactivity as were necessitated by his stationing himself at Rose's bedside. The abnormal deprivation of food and sleep that he was suffering probably contributed by making him tired, and he did add variety to his vigil from time to time by haranguing the nurses or even the doctors. When Rose was awake he would attempt to do her hair, applying a comb and small brush with great gentleness while she lamented that the dye must be growing out and the grey growing in and she hated to think what she looked like. Of course he told her soothingly that it didn't matter at all and she still looked beautiful. He seemed to mean it. He telephoned Millie fairly frequently if only to talk about Rose and more than once drove her to the hospital to visit. Millie was better able to assess the patient's condition than he was and after the third of these visits she warned him that Rose was in fact very ill and unlikely to recover and that he should make up his mind to it. Ted responded with angry tears. Whether he actually believed her but felt she should not have expressed such an idea or whether he imagined she was merely intending to distress him was unclear, but distressed he certainly was. Rose was responding less and less well to the antibiotics, Rachel was present at the bedside more often and Ted reverted to his weeping and protesting with even greater vehemence than before. It was so pervasive as to reach the patients in the general part of the ward and Rose herself finally managed without difficulty to persuade the nursing staff that she could tolerate no more of it.

The charge nurse was consulted and it was decided that a notice should be put on the door of Rose's room ordering all visitors to check with the nursing staff before entering. This was a procedure in place but rarely adopted and the ward was abuzz with the news that it was considered necessary.

"Shouldn't somebody talk to the man first and tell him to be quieter and more sensible?" one of the lesser nurses enquired.

"That was tried earlier and he did seem to be better for a while, but he's been so loud and unreasonable in the last few days it's disturbing everybody, particularly the patient," the charge nurse responded. "We may still have problems when he sees the notice and we'll try and talk to him again then and get the doctor to have a go at him as well."

"What if he refuses to stay out? I've seen what he can be like and I wouldn't be too surprised!"

"We'd have to get Security up to deal with him. I hope it won't come to that. It's usually kept for drunks in A&E!"

When Ted came in the next morning the notice, large and clear and impossible to overlook, was prominent on the side room door. Ted, however, predictably ignored it and went into the room. He simply did not consider that it might be meant for him. The charge nurse, on the watch for this, went in after him and asked him quietly to come out into the waiting room as they needed to speak to him. He obeyed willingly enough, thinking it might have something to do with Rose's condition and the exclusion of new visitors. The charge nurse told him to sit down. "Now Mr - er, Dr - Habgood, isn't it?"

"Yes, that's right." Then anxiously, "She's worse, isn't she?"

"It's not really her condition I want to talk about, except as it's affected by your behaviour. You've been spoken to before about it and recently it's been so bad that the patient has requested that you don't come to the ward any more."

"That's not true! I don't believe it. Rose would never say that. She loves me! I'm her next of kin!" Ted burst out into sobs and tears.

"I'm afraid it is true, Dr Habgood, and I don't think you are her next of kin."

"Yes, I am, I know I am, she said I was, you go and check if you don't believe me!"

"Very well. I'll fetch the notes." Charge-nurse left the room, hoping to give him an opportunity to calm down. She returned after a few minutes and opened the file she was carrying. "Yes, here it is, 'Next of Kin: Mrs Rachel Thompson'."

"I might have known it! That woman! It's that woman! *She's* just put that down. She can't have asked Rose. I know Rose wanted *me*, not her. She told me. That woman's trying to keep me away from her. Well, I won't be kept away. You can't keep me away. I'm going in."

"Now Dr Habgood, we'll have to get Security up here to....." but there was no point in finishing the sentence as Ted charged through the doorway and strode to Rose's room. Charge-nurse hastened to the ward telephone and urgently alerted Security, then followed Ted into the side room. Fortunately, as Rose was asleep, he contented himself with weeping copiously, his whole frame heaving with sobs, clearly trying not to make too much noise, trying to be considerate to Rose even in his distress, unwilling to wake her. By the time Security arrived a very few minutes later, in the form of two large, formidable-looking uniformed men, he could offer little physical resistance as they led him out of the ward.

Not only was the ward abuzz with the news of Ted's forcible banning from the hospital, it was the subject of fascinated conversation and speculation in number nine. Valerie and Mary Ann, both of whom had always been decidedly anti-Ted, had become friendly with Rachel during her sojourn in Rose's flat and expressed neither surprise nor concern. Marjorie, who resented more than a little Rachel's taking over as Rose's best friend, considered their attitude judgemental and smug. She had herself been on the receiving end of Ted's kindness and helpfulness and could hardly agree that the treatment meted out to him was 'just retribution'. Benedicta considered that Rose was probably dangerously ill and was more concerned with the state of her soul on her departure from this world than with the effect of her illness on anybody living in it. She therefore approached Rachel and offered to see to it that Rose was visited by a priest and received the last rites. "After all, she is a Catholic, you know."

"Oh, is she? I didn't know. She used to go to a church sometimes when she lived in Hampshire. I suppose it might be a good idea for you to have some sort of priest go and see her. Thank goodness that wretched Theodore's no longer there. He'd be sure to get in the way and make things difficult."

"I'm afraid he's less sensible than he is sensitive. He can be very, very kind and thoughtful but he lacks discretion, so he does, lacks moderation." Benedicta herself could certainly not be said to have such a fault. She was not sure whether Rachel erred in that direction; she did seem to have an unusually strong dislike of Ted. Benedicta had noted this and reserved judgement. She merely intended to arrange for a priest to visit Rose and leave it at that.

Marjorie, who was becoming less and less in sympathy with the other residents of number nine, was particularly piqued to hear that Benedicta was involved with Rose's spiritual needs. She said as much to Valerie and Mary Ann. "After all," she protested, 'I'm really close to Rose; we spent a lot of time together. She never saw Benedicta half as much. I do think I might have been allowed to arrange a priest for her."

"But you're not a Catholic!" Valerie responded with amazement. "You don't go to church at all!"

Since she had acquired the habit of attending Sunday church on a regular basis Mary Ann felt a decided sense of superiority. "You can't know any priests. Benedicta sees them all the time."

"I could easily have found one. The churches are all in the telephone books and you can find them online, too. It's that Rachel taking over. I hardly even know what's happening now."

Marjorie went up to her own flat and decided to telephone Millie.

"Oh, Millie? It's Marjorie Reed. I wanted to ask you about Theodore, er, Ted. And in fact what's happening generally on that front. Would you like to come and have a drink with me this evening? Or any time soon. Yes, tomorrow would be excellent. You know where it is, of course. My flat's on the top floor."

Millie was surprised at what she regarded as Marjorie's summons, but she was by no means loath to talk about the whole subject of Ted's reaction to Rose's illness with somebody who was clearly interested. She duly made her way to number nine and climbed the stairs to the top floor. They spent the next couple of hours most satisfactorily.

"How is Theodore, do you know? I haven't seen him since he was banned from the hospital. But I thought he looked terrible even before that. He's lost an awful lot of weight."

"Yes, you're right, it is terrible. He won't eat, or drink either, come to that. I've made sandwiches when he's come round to my place and p'raps got him to eat one, but he says food makes him feel sick. And it's not as if he smokes any more. He said Rose was always telling him to stop smoking because 'She didn't want him to die before she did'. Well of course she didn't; she needed him to do a lot of things for her. She'd've been lost without him. He made special bread for her every week and took her shopping all the time. Not to mention fixing things in the flat and helping with her computer. Of course, it's different now she's in hospital."

Marjorie listened with interest and reflected that she herself was also less necessary to Rose than before. Aloud she said "What's he doing now that he can't go to the hospital? And how does his wife feel about all this? She can't be very happy about him making such a fuss over another woman."

"She never talks about it and you can't ask. Do you know we were all due to go on holiday up to the house some of his family used to live in. It's let out for holiday groups to stay in now and their daughter arranges it every year. But *this* year we couldn't go because he couldn't bear to be away from Rose. He did say we could go without him, there'd be other relations there. But we couldn't drive there, it's a long way, right up north, and we'd be stuck there without driving, too. So we didn't go."

"Oh dear! It seems ironical that he can't be with Rose now anyway. It's a pity the ban wasn't in force before you were due to go on holiday."

"I don't think he would have gone anyway. He's never been able to believe it was Rose that had him banned; he's convinced it was all down to Rachel. But I've suspected before now that Rose wasn't always straight with him. I said as much to him once, but it only made him angry."

Marjorie pondered on this without replying. She was unwilling to think badly of Rose but could not fail to realise that her behaviour towards Ted had often been at odds with her comments about him. Finally she said: "Well, he's not very good at taking hints or seeing things from other people's points of view. And of course Rose wouldn't have wanted to hurt his feelings."

"That's true enough I s'pose. About him not taking hints, anyway. He used to buy me a pack of lemon slices every week because I'd once said I liked them. I kept telling him I already had plenty, and even said I'd gone off them. But he still brought a pack every week. I was giving them to all the neighbours and putting them out at the church teas and I got so I never wanted to see another one." Millie sighed. "He does overdo things."

"Do you think it would help if I talked to Rose about how he's suffering?" Marjorie asked. "I can't help feeling sorry for him. He's really been so kind and he does mean well."

"I'm going to see her myself the day after tomorrow. I'll have a go and let you know how I get on if you like; but it'll depend if Rachel's there. I won't dare mention Ted if she is. But look at the time! I never meant to stay so long, I'm ever so sorry, but it's been really helpful."

"Oh, please don't apologise; I'm most grateful to you for coming and I'll look forward to hearing from you again soon."

Millie and Marjorie both derived considerable sat-isfaction from their time together and Millie was in fact fortunate enough to visit Rose at a time when Rachel was not present. She was able to speak sympathetically to Rose about her illness and have a generally soothing and cheering effect before working round to Ted's dejection and dis-tress. Rose rolled her eyes upwards and sighed and finally said that perhaps he could come in just once as long as he brought his wife with him. Mil-lie wondered whether this was something Rose considered unlikely to happen and was a clever method of appearing to give way while in fact making a visit from Ted pretty impossible. Surely Emily would find it too demeaning and embar-rassing. Any wife surely would in such circum-stances. Nevertheless Millie made the most of the supposed concession by asking if Rose would like her to tell the charge-nurse.

Rose replied faintly "Oh yes, I suppose you can. But only on that condition, mind."

Millie was well accustomed to visiting the sick and in no awe of hospitals and their staff. She had a productive chat with the charge-nurse, who was, fortunately, not the one who had summoned Se-curity to deal with Ted's ejection from the ward. She had of course heard of the incident and had al-ways considered that she would have dealt with it considerably better herself. She would never have let things come to such a pass in the first place! This she made clear to Millie, who expressed herself in complete agreement, and they parted with very satisfactory feelings of mutual approval.

CHAPTER 13

To everybody's astonishment Emily accompanied her husband to the hospital to see Rose. Rose herself was probably more astonished than anybody. True, she had always been on perfectly good terms with Emily and they had seen each other not infrequently in the past at college dinners and other inclusive occasions, but never previously in the hospital as Ted had come only on his own or occasionally with Millie.

Other patients became rather neglected as the nursing staff gathered at the nurses' station to discuss the matter in hushed tones. A senior nurse volunteered to 'go and see if they're all right'. She returned to report that 'he' was actually doing Rose's hair with a brush and comb while 'the other woman' was standing there holding hair clips or something.

"It's his wife, you know, the other woman!" charge-nurse informed her.

"I can't believe it. How must she feel about the way he goes on over Rose?" the senior nurse queried incredulously.

"It doesn't look as if she feels anything. But at least

he's not making any fuss at the moment, he's not even crying. He used to be in a terrible state most of the time, didn't he?"

"P'raps he's too scared of being banned again. Or maybe his wife never knew what he's been like. But she must know about him being banned and only allowed to come here if she came too. I'd never've bloody come if I'd've been his wife, would you?"

There was general agreement that no, they wouldn't've. "And there she is," the senior nurse continued, "standing there while he does another woman's hair!"

"Pity he doesn't do something about his wife's hair," one of the younger nurses commented. "Did you see it? Just tied all anyhow with a rubber band and a wiggly parting and wisps all over the place. Can't have been cut for years. Not too surprising he likes somebody else better!"

There was a general giggly agreement with this until an older, African nurse spoke firmly. "Well I think she's got a very sweet face and she's a very brave woman. She must know everybody's going to stare at her and talk about it all."

"Quite right, Malawa," the charge-nurse recollected herself. "Get back to the other patients, the rest of you. We can't all stand round here gossiping. I'm going to send them away in a few minutes anyhow. They're only going to be allowed a short visit. There would have been a lot less trouble if that had been enforced from the start!"

Ted and Emily left the hospital without any fuss after being required to do so and warned that they must telephone in advance and seek permission before coming again. Ted merely looked distant and distressed and said nothing but Emily readily agreed and thanked the charge- nurse cheerfully and politely. She made a very good impression and those of the staff who saw the encounter were in-clined to agree with Nurse Malawa's assessment of her. Ted dropped her at home and then went to tell Millie all about the visit.

He let himself in, calling "Hullo, it's me!" as usual. Millie was in the kitchen making sandwiches.

"I thought you'd be coming in," she said in her usual, sensible tones, "and I'm making you some sandwiches. Now eat them and have something to drink."

"No, I can't. I don't want anything. The thought of food makes me feel sick."

"Of course you feel sick if you don't eat. Here's a cup of tea to start with and you've to have one sandwich if you like it or not. I haven't made them for nothing." She put the tea and one sandwich down in front of him. "Go on, eat it!"

Ted drank the tea quite gratefully. It was well laced with full cream milk and several spoonsful of sugar so it was a good beginning. After half a cup he did in fact pick up the sandwich and take a bite. It was of thin white bread and filled with meat paste and tomato and not heavy or unappetising. Even so, Ted seemed to have some difficulty swallowing it, but he washed it down with the rest of the tea.

Millie filled the cup again. "Have this and finish the sandwich," she demanded. Ted gave a loud sigh and took a sip of tea.

"Now tell me how it went," Millie demanded.

"We did her hair. She was pleased with that. They didn't let us stay very long and we have to ring up before we can go again. Emily spoke to the charge-nurse. It was a different one."

"Well, don't tempt fate by ringing up too soon."

"No, I won't; and Emily can't come for a few days and I can only go if I'm with her. It's all Rachel's doing, you know. Rose would never have had me banned."

Millie merely murmured "Hmmm", which Ted took for agreement, but which in fact meant quite the opposite. Millie had emailed one of the doctors in whose practice she had once worked to ask him whether it was possible for anybody other than the patient to have a person banned from seeing them in hospital. She had received a fairly detailed reply explaining the whole process and making it clear that only the patient could set it in motion. She was very tempted to point this out to Ted in the hope of undermining his devotion to Rose and giving him some realisation that it was not entirely well placed; but she was not sure whether this would add to his suffering rather than diminish it. She decided reluctantly that her non-committal murmur was probably the safest response.

It was three days later when Millie received a telephone call in the middle of the morning. It was Ted. He spoke without preamble. "Rose died last night," he said. To Millie's surprise he didn't seem to be weeping.

"Oh!" she replied. "Oh dear! I'm very sorry. Have you just heard?"

"Yes, and I wouldn't have but I telephoned her solicitor to ask about getting me put down as next of kin for Mrs Rose Thorneycroft and he said 'Ah, the *late* Mrs Thorneycroft!' So that's how I knew; the only way I knew. Nobody thought to even let me know she was dying. I should have been with her." Here Ted did begin to weep as his distress overcame his anger.

"I don't suppose you know yet when the funeral is?" Millie sought to take refuge in practical details.

"No, I don't even know that. I asked the solicitor and he said Mrs Rachel Thompson was seeing to it all and as far as he knew it was to be a completely private cremation with a memorial service later on. It's terrible." Ted broke down completely, said a muffled 'Goodbye' and hung up. Millie sighed, realised that there was nothing she could do and went about her usual household business, confident that Ted would soon be round to see her.

The inhabitants of number nine learned of Rose's death rather before Ted did, as Rachel informed her newly acquired friend Valerie, who informed Mary Ann, who informed Benedicta, who hesitated to inform Marjorie as Marjorie had not spoken to her since she had had the temerity to usurp Marjorie's supposed reign as Rose's best friend by summoning a priest to attend Rose in hospital. Fortunately she had done so in good time so that Rose had not departed from this world 'unhouseled, unannealed' but had apparently been able to die a good death, whatever sins of omission and commission she had committed in this life. Benedicta was satisfied that this was the case for, as she remarked to Mary Ann when she enquired about it, "Rose hadn't really lapsed, she used to come to mass with me sometimes. She just hadn't quite settled anywhere she wanted to go in Oxford."

So Marjorie was the only member of the household to remain uninformed, a fact which subsequently did not greatly improve her opinion of the other occupants of number nine. She heard the news only when she telephoned Millie to ask if she knew how Ted was. She realised, of course, that Rachel must have been the first to know and was particularly distressed and displeased that the information had not been immediately given to her;

had not, in fact, been given to her at all. Seeking an ally she rang Ted and commiserated with him. Though he broke down frequently he managed to convey a good deal about his enemy Rachel Thompson, whom he regarded as the sole cause of his grievances, an attitude with which Marjorie was in considerable agreement and sympathy.

Many articles in Rose's flat actually belonged to Ted, among them a television set and a computer, as well as some kitchen appliances, which he had supplied for her use, or at least *his* use when cooking for her. There were other things for which he had a sentimental fondness as she had always said he could have them whenever he liked: an oil painted by a friend of hers and a clock, which he had cleaned, restored and made to work so well that it actually kept very good time. He tried to contact Rachel about these things both by email and by letter, but received no reply. The thing he was most particularly anxious to acquire, however, was Rose's car. Not only did he really need it, as his own car was very old and very untrustworthy, but he had driven her many many miles in hers and felt as deeply attached to it as if it contained something of her presence. He was, of course, perfectly willing to pay for it, and indeed for anything else he was anxious to possess, and resorted to contacting Rose's solicitor to negotiate any necessary proceedings. The solicitor, who knew Ted quite well from the times when he had accompanied Rose on visits to him, was sympathetic, but made it clear that he was baulked at every turn by Rachel Thompson, who was executor of the will and seemed to have control of everything. Ted was in despair and let his distress be known to anybody who would listen. Marjorie was one of his chief sympathisers and through her the news of his grievances reached all the inhabitants of number nine and any of their acquaintances who might be interested. Rachel retaliated by accusing Ted of illegally entering Rose's flat and taking anything and everything he wanted. Her friend Valerie had no hesitation in believing this of Ted and Mary Ann was inclined to think it not improbable. Even Benedicta, who remembered Ted entering her flat with a key taken from its hiding place and without warning, was not entirely unwilling to believe it. Only Marjorie, who had after all known him for a number of years, was adamant in declaring it to be totally false and in roundly declaring as much to Valerie.

"It's absolutely libellous," she stated firmly, having gone to Valerie's flat with the determined purpose of telling her so, "and you should be more careful about what you're saying."

Valerie was so convinced of Rachel's integrity and so hostile to Ted that she went so far as to telephone an acquaintance of hers who had, she knew, been an associate of Ted's for a number of years. "What do you know about this Theodore Habgood?" she demanded with little preamble and in a tone which conveyed a considerable degree of angry disapproval. The acquaintance was unsurprisingly taken aback and not unreasonably asked the purpose of the inquiry. Valerie gave a brief and decidedly biased account of the situation. She did not find the reaction particularly rewarding.

"Well, really! Ted Habgood! I know he's inclined to be silly about women, but I'd swear on oath that he's scrupulously honest. Nobody who knew him could possibly accuse him of theft of any kind. Anybody who does must have some particularly spiteful motivation. I'd check out on that if I were you!"

Valerie had at least the good sense to feel a small qualm at the thought of her own motivation and a small doubt as to the fairness of Rachel's accusations, so she managed to thank the recipient of her call with a reasonably good grace though without acknowledging any alteration in her own opinion.

Ted never received the clock or the picture or any of the kitchen things but the television set and the computer were restored to him, delivered to his house in fact, presumably so that he would have no excuse to enter the flat himself. These were the things he cared least about; what most particularly distressed him was his loss of the car. Some few days later, however, Marjorie was interrupted, when conducting an early evening session with an informal drama group she was running, by a frantic knocking on the door of her flat. It was Ted. "I need help; you've got to help me; please!" he burst out as she opened the door.

"Whatever's the matter?"

"It's the car. Please, drive me up to get it. It's at a garage where it's been sold for scrap. I've got to get it now before Rachel stops me."

"Now? But I'm taking a class, leading a group. Surely she can't stop you if the car's already been sold to a garage."

"She can. She will if I don't go and get it now. Please help me."

Marjorie could see that Ted was quite desperate and would be impossible to put off. He would only come in and disrupt the class if she refused and she hadn't the heart to shut the door on him. "All right; go and wait in the car park; I'll come down as soon as I've dealt with my class."

She returned to her sitting room and told the assembled group, who had clearly heard, however indistinctly, that some emergency had arisen, that she had to go and help a friend in distress and could they continue on their own until she came back. As they were doing a play reading this was not too difficult and they agreed readily. Of course they spent the time immediately after her departure putting together the snippets they had heard and conjecturing what might be the cause of the sudden emergency. It was with some reluctance that they settled back to the play reading.

In the car park Ted was pacing up and down. He insisted on driving Marjorie's car himself and they arrived at the garage, some little way out of Oxford, in a remarkably short time thanks to Ted's impatient haste. Once there he thanked Marjorie with more brevity than politeness and rushed into the building, leaving her to find her way home as best she could. By now it was dark and she was unfamiliar with the area and by no means sure which way to go. Cursing the selfishness of men she set off and almost immediately found herself on a ring road with signs that seemed to say anything but Oxford. She had horrible visions of coming to somewhere distant and unknown and running out of petrol. In fact this awful anxiety was quite unfounded and the next sign on the road clearly showed a turn off to Oxford, but she did take rather longer to get home than she had hoped and was feeling increasingly uncharitable towards Ted as the car clock increased its numbers.

By the time she reached her flat several members of the drama group had left and the few remaining did not trouble to inform her that they had not actually finished reading the play and merely said soothingly that everything had gone perfectly well and they could all make up for any lost time at the next meeting. Marjorie was relieved to see them depart. She closed the door thankfully, considered making herself a cup of tea and decided that a good sized tot of brandy would be far more suitable in the circumstances. It was undoubtedly the right decision; she even felt almost kindly towards Ted by the time he rang some half hour later, though she was at first somewhat puzzled as to what he was ringing about.

"You won't tell them, will you?" he said urgently, "make sure you don't tell them!"

"Tell who? What?"

"Tell them I've got the car. If Rachel knows she'll try to get it away from me!"

"Now really, Ted, that's simply not possible. I presume you've paid for it, haven't you?"

"Yes of course I have."

"Well then, it's now legally yours and can't be taken from you. You don't imagine Rachel's going to come to your place and drive it away, do you?"

"I wouldn't put it past her."

"Has she got a key to it?"

"She might have, for all I know."

"Now that's ridiculous. She'd be charged with theft if she took it. Besides, she doesn't even know you've bought it."

"No; not unless you tell her, tell any of them; that's what I'm worried about. You won't tell them, will you?"

"No of course I won't. I'm not on the best of terms with them, anyway. And I think you've been very cruelly treated."

Ted seemed satisfied with Marjorie's assurances. He had rung from outside Millie's house and now went inside it to tell her in detail what had happened. Marjorie decided to go to bed but found it difficult to sleep. She mulled over Ted's surely irrational fears and behaviour and feared he was on the verge of a breakdown, if not already in the throes of it. Rachel was certainly not in Rose's flat, which was now completely devoid of furniture; she was most unlikely even to be in Oxford. The idea that she could have in any way prevented him from purchasing a car which had already been sold to a garage was really grotesque. It was true that Rachel's refusal to allow it to be sold to him savoured of spiteful malice, but that must be the end of her influence in the matter. She hoped he would see things more rationally in the morning and composed herself sufficiently to doze into a sleep.

CHAPTER 14

The next day began with Valerie seeing Ted's ancient car in its erstwhile place - in *her* allocated car space. She felt quite a jolt, as if it was a ghost from the past. "I hope I'm not seeing things!" she murmured to herself. She went and made a cup of tea and then looked out again. There was no mistaking that car, and it was still there. She drank the tea slowly and decided to ring Mary Ann and see if she knew anything about it. Mary Ann was uninformed but by no means uninterested. She considered the matter briefly and began to work out a possible explanation, speaking her thoughts as they came to her.

"Well, there's only one person in this house who's at all sympathetic with that Theodore, isn't there?"

"Marjorie, of course," Valerie responded.

"Do you suppose she's stepping into Rose's shoes? She's known Theodore for a long time herself. Do you think she might be *consoling* him?"

"Good grief, what a thought! It's surely not possible!"

Mary Ann gave a little giggle "Good *grief* indeed! You must admit it *is* possible. After all, he can't have stayed in Rose's flat, it's completely bare and empty. And how could he have got in?"

"Rachel seemed to think he had a key, so he probably could have. But could he have been there all night?"

"I think it's more probable that he was with Marjorie." Mary Ann was inclined to favour the theory she had herself come up with. "I'll try and find out from her, though she hasn't been very friendly lately."

"I think she's less against you than against the rest of us. She's annoyed with Benedicta and she knows I'm very friendly with Rachel, so you'd be the best person. Let me know how you get on!"

"I don't suppose I can do any more than you can at the moment; after all he must still be here seeing his car's here. I know, though: I'll ring Marjorie and ask her to come and have coffee with me and see if she makes excuses."

Mary Ann prefaced her invitation with a kind enquiry as to Marjorie's wellbeing and the sympathetic expectation that she must be missing Rose sadly. Marjorie, rather touched at this, responded with some gratitude that she really would appreciate a cup of coffee. As she put down the telephone Mary Ann reflected unwillingly that it somehow didn't *seem* as if Marjorie had anybody else there. One could usually *tell* if a person were speaking on the telephone when they were not alone; they always *sounded* different.

Marjorie descended to Mary Ann's flat very promptly and wafted in rather dramatically; her distress at Rose's death was certainly very apparent. Mary Ann fussed over her sympathetically as if her right to be treated as a grieving bereaved was unquestionable. Marjorie responded with gratitude and expressed her hurt at being the last to know of Rose's death and her inability even to attend the funeral, which seemed to have taken place almost in secret. Mary Ann replied soothingly that this was indeed very strange, but that there would be a memorial service they could all go to, and as to hearing of the death itself, well of course everybody supposed that Marjorie would have been the first to know. "After all," Mary Ann concluded, "you know Theodore quite well, don't you, and he must have known."

"No, as a matter of fact he didn't. He's very unhappy about it. He only heard at all because he happened to telephone Rose's solicitor. I fear it's made things even worse for him. He won't eat and can hardly be persuaded to have so much as a cup of tea. He's really not very well."

"I see his car's here again," Mary Ann seized the opportunity to broach the subject.

"Oh? Can you see it from here?" Marjorie was aware that the explanation of the car's presence was not an option if she were to keep her promise to Ted. She would have to tread warily. She also became aware that there was rather more behind Mary Ann's invitation to coffee than an unusual effusion of human kindness.

Mary Ann was somewhat thrown by Marjorie's question because in fact she was not able to see the car park from her flat and she certainly didn't want to admit to having discussed the matter with Valerie. "Oh, ah, when I was outside earlier – but it may not be there now. It seemed strange; he surely can't be, er, have been, in Rose's flat, it's empty."

"Valerie won't be pleased," Marjorie observed, "if he parks in her space again. She always felt strongly about it." She felt something like triumph at the ease with which she had avoided any admission of knowledge about the presence of Ted and his car and decided to drain her coffee cup and make her farewells immediately before Mary Ann could ask any more questions. She managed to get as far as the door and open it but was unable to go through it as the doorway was filled by Valerie's not inconsiderable bulk. They both exclaimed simultaneously, but neither was willing to give way and they both held their ground.

"Oh, you're still here!" was Valerie's not very tactful comment.

Mary Ann did her best to rectify things by saying, in tones that implied she was giving previously unknown information, "Marjorie's just been to have coffee with me!"

"Well, can you tell me anything about that car of your friend Theodore's? It seems to have been here all night!" Valerie was clearly addressing Marjorie, whom she was literally confronting and with whom she would have been closely face to face, had not Marjorie been considerably taller than she was.

Hardly feeling her height an advantage, Marjorie took a step backwards and countered "Why do you suppose I should know anything about it?"

"It's obvious, isn't it? You've always been on his side and against Rachel. I suppose he's seeing *you* now that Rose is no longer with us. He's the sort that can't do without seeing *somebody*."

"You're being completely ridiculous. Kindly let me pass. I can see now why I was invited to coffee; but at least Mary Ann hasn't insulted me even if she is in cahoots with you." Marjorie stepped forward with such vigour that Valerie had to give way, allowing her to reach unimpeded the staircase to her own flat.

"Oh dear!" Mary Ann's voice rose almost to a wail. "She'll never trust me again! It's all too awful. We never used to be like this. Rose's death seems to have put us all at odds."

"It's that Theodore's fault. He's the one who's caused all the trouble. Look at the way he behaved in the hospital. He always went on as if he owned the place, as well as owning Rose. He can't be sane."

"Well, Marjorie did say she thought he was ill, I mean mentally ill, because apparently he won't eat or drink and he's lost an awful lot of weight."

"Hmph!" Valerie was not impressed. "He must be eating something or he wouldn't survive. It's probably all part of a ploy to make people feel sorry for him. He's got a personality disorder, that's his real problem. But what's that noise?"

As they stopped talking they could clearly hear the sound of a car being driven on the gravel outside; they went to the window in time to see Ted's car going out of the gateway.

"Well, thank goodness for that, anyway!" Valerie sank into a chair. "Have you got any coffee left?" she asked.

"Yes, Marjorie only had one cup. You're welcome to finish it up." Mary Ann fetched a clean cup and poured the coffee. "Now I wonder," she pondered aloud, "I wonder if he was in Marjorie's flat all the time and only left when she told him to after she'd been here."

"We didn't hear anybody come down the stairs though," Valerie was doubtful.

Mary Ann forbore to press the point but, unwilling to relinquish her theory as to Marjorie's involve-ment with Ted, she simply resolved to mull over the matter with her friend Clarissa Hillman, per-haps with the help of a good tea at the Randolph or

The Feathers in Woodstock.

Ted drove his old car as far as Millie's house and let himself in. "Hullo love," he called as usual. "It's me!"

"I'm upstairs," Millie responded. "Just coming down. Put the kettle on."

"I don't want any tea," was Ted's immediate response.

"Well I do." Millie went into the kitchen and put the kettle on herself. Ted sat in the sitting room.

"I've brought the old car back. I didn't see anybody," he called.

"Did they see you, though?" Millie spoke from the door of the sitting room. "They must have thought you'd been there all night."

"Why? What do you mean?"

"Well, if the car was there all night they must have thought you were, too. They don't know you've got Rose's car, do they? And after all, it isn't the first time."

"What isn't the first time?"

"The first time you've been there all night."

"That's not true. I've told you before. I really loved Rose but it wasn't sex!"

"I thought you said it wasn't *just* sex."

"No, I didn't. You're making it up. You're trying to cheapen the whole thing. Rose was *special.* She was the cleverest woman I've ever known."

"I thought you said she was worse than me on the computer!"

"That's not what I meant! She knew about everything. She could do crosswords. I showed her how to do Sudokus and she caught on straightaway. You're trying to demean her. I'm not staying to hear it." Ted almost flung himself out of the house.

Millie could hear him start his car with a snort and a roar. She cast her eyes to heaven and hoped he'd get home without hitting anything. Nevertheless there was nothing she could usefully do about him so she finished making the sandwiches she'd hoped she might have persuaded him to eat, made a good, strong pot of tea to go with them and ate them herself.

CHAPTER 15

Standing in her kitchen Valerie heard the particularly noisy engine of a car apparently driven at speed into the car park at the back of the house. "If that's that Theodore again!" she murmured angrily to herself as she looked out of the window. But it was not 'that Theodore' or any car associated with him, it was a small green car of an even older vintage; in fact, she realised with considerable surprise, a Morris Minor! It stopped with an almost violent jolt in the space belonging to the flat formerly occupied by Rose. Out of it came a small, sinewy-looking, elderly woman, who slammed the car door fiercely and advanced on the house with the kind of swiftly determined gait that matched her driving. "Heavens!" Valerie murmured to herself, "don't tell me that's the new tenant coming into Rose's flat!"

She considered which of her housemates might have any up-to-date information on the matter, rejected Marjorie, with whom she was hardly on speaking terms after their last encounter; decided against Mary Ann, whom she considered a rather less than accurate informant, and finally rang

Benedicta. This proved to be a profitable decision as Benedicta answered her query with: "Yes, and she's here with me now, so she is; come down and meet her."

Valerie was delighted to comply and become acquainted with the energetic little woman she'd seen in the car park, introduced by Benedicta as "Martha Prout; we know each other from church. I told her about Rose's flat and I'm glad to say she's decided to take it as from next week."

Martha shook hands with vigour and Marjorie asked her if she'd known Rose too.

"Well, I'd met her once or twice when she came to Blackfriars with Benedicta, but she never seemed very keen to talk to me. Tried to make friends. Asked her to come to a coffee morning at the Oratory; meet some other ladies our sort of age. She never came. Don't think she liked me much. She came from Argentina, too. I know it well; used to be very involved with a mission there — looking after street children; very exciting, very dangerous. Had to carry a gun. Too old now. Had to leave it to the Jesuits to cope with. Sad really. Don't know what to do with myself without it. Oh well, moving into a new flat; keep me busy for a day or two. Glad to meet a house mate. Must be off now, though; lot to see to. Going upstairs to case the joint. Got the keys. Goodbye." She was up the steep stairs and out of the door before Benedicta had reached the third step. Valerie looked on with some wonder; she'd always considered Benedicta remarkably active and energetic for her age, but she was no match for Martha Prout.

"Wow!" she exclaimed as Benedicta came and sat down again. "What a ball of energy! I can't believe she thinks she's too old for anything."

"Och, it's not herself that thinks so. It's the Jesuits that have taken over from her. A bit of a loose cannon they thought she was, and a bit too careless and too hopeful where it came to money."

"She could hardly be more different from Rose!" "Now there you're truly right!"

Valerie left Benedicta's flat and on her way upstairs called in on Mary Ann to impart the news of Martha Prout's arrival. Mary Ann was rewardingly interested.

"Now I *am* pleased to hear that!" was her immediate response. "It's been quite depressing having that flat empty and unoccupied; it made it seem *dead*, don't you think, dead, like Rose. We need something different to think about and nothing else seemed to be happening."

"Well, we've got Rose's Memorial Service coming up," Valerie demurred, "that's something to think about."

"It's not exactly something different. And there's the problem of who's going with *whom*! That's going to be difficult with all the feuding that's been going on. I mean, who will Marjorie go with?"

Valerie gave a sound between a laugh and a grunt. "Well not with *me,* that's for sure. But I don't mind taking you and Benedicta."

"Oh dear! Poor Marjorie. She'll feel even more hostile towards us. It does seem a shame."

"Hmph! She'll probably go with that Theodore and his lot. Anyway, it's not for a couple of weeks yet. Shall we do anything about welcoming this Martha Prout?"

"Oh now that *is* a good idea." Mary Ann spoke with something like relief. "I don't mind having everybody here and I can ask Marjorie *especially* and perhaps *mollify* her a little."

The impact of Martha Prout's move into number nine was not inconsiderable. The other inhabitants regarded her with interest and a mixture of alarm and admiration at her display of energy. Benedicta achieved a certain amount of limelight from having previous knowledge of her and the general atmosphere improved as the factions engendered by the circumstances of Rose's death became less paramount. Mary Ann had a modest wine and nibbles gathering for all the occupants of the house. She ordered the food from Waitrose and Valerie came early to help with the wine so it was not too difficult even though, as she remarked to her helper, she didn't have a *cavalier servente* to assist her!

"I can't imagine our new housemate's likely to have one, either!" was Valerie's comment.

Mary Ann responded with her usual giggle and then remembered that they needed another glass because she'd forgotten to say that she'd invited her friend Clarissa from church, "because I've told her so much about us all and of course she knows Ted — Theodore — and she's really interested to meet everybody. I think she quite envies me living in a house like this with my own space but lots of interest and other people. She lives with a husband fifteen years older than she is and *reclusive;* he sounds *very* boring! So really she has the worst of both worlds. Sometimes I think there's quite a lot to be said for being rid of one's husband, don't you think so?"

"Maybe for somebody like you who had a rich one!" Valerie had had to work for some years after her divorce and still found herself less well off than she would have liked. "Is Martha Prout divorced, do you know?"

"I don't know. I've seen letters to her addressed to *Mrs* M. Prout so I suppose she must have been married; otherwise I might not have thought so. She seems so independent."

"Well, she wears a wedding ring; but she could have done that for safety's sake if she lived in Argentina. Anyway — oh there's your doorbell!"

The guests arrived simultaneously and the party started. Only Clarissa needed introducing and as she knew all the names already and could soon attach them to the right people, thanks to Mary Ann's vivid briefing, she had little difficulty in remembering who was who. The guest of honour was in the habit of touring the country giving lectures — and appeals for donations — on her charity work in Argentina, so had no inhibitions about holding the floor, despite her small stature.

"So glad to see you all. Good of you. Feel I know you already. Yes thanks, move going pretty well. Haven't got much. No fancy furniture. Some of it's collapsible: garden chair sort of thing; card table. Easy to manage. Lots of paper: all in filing cabinets. No trouble to removal men. Won't have anything to do by next week. Church work, of course, if I can help the Blackfriars with anything. Benedicta does a lot. Mass every day, of course. Have to find something else to do as well, though. Oh" to Clarissa, "don't know you, do I? Friend of somebody's? Oh, organist at the church Mary Ann goes to. Good for you. Yes, another glass of red, thank you. Nice food. Won't need any supper. Yes, some family in England; brother a priest. Lives in Staffordshire. Daughter in Spain; well last time I heard from her. Moves about a lot. Hard to keep track of her. Do my best. Grandson works on a farm; north of England."

This lively spate of information was maintained for some time longer than most of the audience could take it in, but it undeniably kept the party going and a generous amount of good food and drink heightened the atmosphere. By the time the guests left they were all decidedly elated and feeling more generally charitable to one another than was invariably the case. Even Valerie and Marjorie had managed to exchange a few words, though they were careful not to depart at precisely the same time. Clarissa stayed on ostensibly to help Mary Ann, though in fact they both collapsed on to easy chairs with 'a bottle we might as well finish' and conducted a *post mortem* on the party, leaving the empty glasses where they stood and the plates where they lay.

The slight lightening of tension in the house, which the party in Mary Ann's flat had helped to establish, seemed to be maintained and even aided by Martha's presence. She treated everybody in exactly the same way and was not unlike a younger, more sprightly version of Benedicta, without having fallen out with Marjorie or anybody else. Marjorie was still considering that *she* should have been asked to find a priest to attend Rose's death bed and was still convinced that *she* had been Rose's best friend by far, however unfairly ousted by Rachel Thompson. Valerie's friendship with the latter did not ameliorate Marjorie's opinion of either of them, though she did manage to make peace with Mary Ann. She still missed Rose sorely. The fact that all the other occupants of number nine were to go to Rose's Memorial Service together increased her feeling of isolation. Even Martha was to go, in Valerie's car along with Mary Ann and Benedicta. She had at first been decidedly unwilling to do so but had been persuaded by Benedicta and Mary Ann, who had deliberately convinced her, over a *special* cup of morning coffee in a coffee bar in Summertown, of the *enormous help* her presence would be to them. "*Because* you see, it will be obvious if you come that there simply isn't *room* in Valerie's car for Marjorie. So it won't look so bad that she's *not included.*" Mary Ann had genuine sympathy for Marjorie but was also keen to avoid what she privately called 'any vulgar display of animosity' either from Valerie or from Rachel Thompson when they met her. Marjorie was undeniably of the 'Theodore camp' to which Valerie and Rachel were bitterly opposed.

Benedicta sighed and agreed. "It's a sad thing that the death of somebody we all liked should result in such conflict as it truly has, God forgive us. You'll be something of a neutral presence, Martha, so you will. And you did know the woman."

"Knew she didn't like me!" Martha objected.

"But did *you* not like *her?*" Mary Ann wanted to know.

"Never thought much about her. Seemed friendly enough with other people. Wondered why not with me. Not important. Other things to think about. Really want me to come, do you?"

The combined assurances of Benedicta and Mary

154

Ann had their effect and Martha did also have some curiosity to meet Rachel Thompson, who seemed from what she had heard to have been the main cause of dissension. "Right. I'll come. Tell Valerie."

CHAPTER 16

The day of the Memorial Service arrived. Marjorie was, as Valerie had predicted, to travel with Ted, Emily and Millie in the car which they all described as 'Rose's car'. Valerie had, of course, not been entirely sure who 'Ted and his lot' as she had described them, comprised, and she certainly had no idea that the car in which they were to travel was not the 'dreadful old banger' he had always driven but the one which had belonged to Rose! Marjorie reflected that her housemates in general and Rachel Thompson in particular might be more than a little surprised to see them all in the car she had sold off as scrap to an out of town garage in her determination that Ted was not to have it!

Ted arrived early, before Valerie had left her flat, and drove, as he always had done, into her parking space as her car was as usual out on the road. She saw the newly arrived vehicle as she looked out of her kitchen window, recognised it as Rose's car, gasped with horror and really believed for more than a minute that she was indeed 'seeing things'! She stood at the window unable to move. Then the telephone rang and she told herself to be sensible and answer it. It was Mary Ann asking if Valerie were ready to take her.

"Oh," she answered, "yes, yes of course. I'll be down in a second."

"Are you all right?" Mary Ann enquired, "You sound — well —shocked!"

"It's Rose's car!" Valerie replied.

"What? What is? Whatever do you mean?"

"In my parking space. Rose's car. Rachel had it taken away to a garage for scrap. It's here!"

"It can't be. It must be one like it."

"No. I remember the number. I'm good at numbers."

"Well we're still going in yours, aren't we?"

"Yes. Yes of course. I'm ready. I was just checking the kitchen when I saw it. I'm coming down now."

So Valerie went to her car and let Mary Ann into it and Benedicta, who hobbled along at the same time, and Martha, who was there already. So she didn't see Theodore emerge from the car which had belonged to Rose and was still completely mystified and not a little perturbed at its unexpected presence.

Theodore left for Hampshire some ten or fifteen minutes later than Valerie and her carload but he drove faster and of course knew the road a great deal better than she did and so, unsurprisingly, arrived at the church rather earlier. When Valerie drove into the nearby parking area the first thing she saw was 'Rose's car'!

"No! I don't believe it!" she exclaimed. "It's *here!*"

"What's here? What's the matter?" Benedicta was puzzled. "Is something wrong with the

place? It seems to be near the church."

"No, the *car!*" Valerie was beginning to feel haunted.

Mary Ann realised what she meant as she was staring in disbelief at the nearest stationary vehicle. "Oh, is that Rose's car? The one you saw at the house this morning?"

"Yes, of course it is!" Valerie was impatient at her passengers' lack of perception. "Surely you know it!"

"But it's been disposed of, surely to goodness?" Benedicta knew the story of the selling for scrap.

Mary Ann outlined it briefly for Martha's benefit, but little explanation was necessary as Martha had in fact heard about it before. "That car doesn't look like scrap, if you mean the one you're staring at, ordinary silver-grey Peugeot. Clearly been driven as far as we have; arrived here before us, too. Anybody else from our place coming to the service?"

"Only Marjorie."

"Driving herself?" Martha wanted to know.

"She can't have been." Valerie was definite. "She

never drives any sort of distance these days. I thought she'd be coming with that Theodore!"

"Obvious then. Picked her up in the Peugeot. Wanted it, didn't he? Must have got it."

"But how *can* he have got it? Rachel couldn't bear the idea of him having it." Valerie had several times listened to Rachel's vehemence on this subject.

"Sounds unreasonable. Why shouldn't he have it? Didn't want it herself. Spiteful, wasn't it?"

Nobody answered this. Benedicta was inclined to agree and even Valerie had to admit to herself that Rachel had behaved rather oddly. After all, she could surely have got a better price from Theodore than she did from the garage. Mary Ann considered such a display of hostility decidedly vulgar. She had always disapproved of Theodore and had thus been of the anti-Theodore camp, but she was by no means impressed with Rachel, whom she had already labelled as NOSP - 'not our sort of person'. The 'our' had originally denoted herself and her family as the expression had been frequently used by her mother. 'My' would have been more appropriate to Mary Ann's present single state, but she mentally supplied the plurality with a largely mythical cohort of 'well-connected' and impeccably *comme il faut* friends and relations.

They progressed to the church, where Rachel was standing at the door to meet and greet them. Martha, who had not seen her before, hung back a little to take in an impression of a rather dumpy, plain woman of at least seventy-five, with a florid complexion and dyed red hair, wearing unbecoming clothes of dark grey and black and an expression of patient fortitude. She handed to each one a small booklet with a cover depicting a large, pink rose and murmured "Thank you for coming" in tones of distressed gratitude. They made their way in and sat in a pew from where they could see, on the opposite side and further towards the front, Marjorie, Theodore, Millie and Emily. Mary Ann knew who they all were and whispered the information to Valerie, who relayed it to Benedicta and Martha. Theodore turned round and stared at them and similarly informed his companions as to the identity of Benedicta, but he didn't know Martha and had to be enlightened by Marjorie, who had hardly expected to see her there.

As they were early and it would be some time before the service actually began they started reading the booklets provided. These immediately elicited whispered exclamations of astonished disbelief. Details of Rose's life were outlined and none of these seemed to correspond with anything either of the Oxford groups had previously heard about it. The entrance of numbers of the local contingent of mourners made enough noise to render almost inaudible the heavily breathed gasps of "No! *That's* not right!" "What nonsense!" "Surely not!" "That *can't* be true!" emerging from

Mary Ann, Valerie and Benedicta. Martha regarded them with interest. She had heard enough of their version of the story of Rose's life to be well aware that it was at odds with almost everything in the booklet. Subsequent discussion, she decided, would hold fascinating possibilities of a mystery to solve. Now, however, the organ was playing and there was no time to go into the matter. All that could be exchanged were astonished glances under raised eyebrows. A woman in clerical clothes advanced to the front of the church; the organ stopped. A welcome was given and a hymn announced and the congregation stood up to sing it.

It was a modern hymn about morning having broken like the first morning and a blackbird having spoken like the first bird. Martha wondered in what way it could be considered at all appropriate to the present occasion and Emily, who had a degree in Zoology, couldn't help thinking that the first bird was probably much more like a dinosaur than a blackbird, while even Ted, who was torn between admiring everything to do with Rose and detesting everything to do with Rachel, was considering that the morning immediately following the Big Bang was unlikely to have been very similar to the one they were enjoying in the green calm of the English countryside.

The hymn over, the clergywoman explained that the Service of Thanksgiving for the life of Rose

Thorneycroft was on the very same day of the year on which Rose's husband had been laid to rest five years earlier. It was, moreover, the same day of the year as their wedding anniversary. So what could be more appropriate than that this devoted couple should be commemorated together, especially as the memorial service always intended for Rose's husband had somehow never taken place.

At the mention of the 'devoted couple' the eyebrows of the inhabitants of number nine were raised in amazement; at the news of the perpetually deferred memorial service they were lowered.

The female vicar went on to outline Rose's life much as it appeared in the rose adorned booklet. "Rose was a very private person and few people will know that she was born in Birmingham, where she went to school, and that she studied languages at Girton College Cambridge. She then taught at girls' schools in Birmingham and Worcester before going to Spain for a year as a teacher. After that she lived in London with her friend Siobhan O'Halloran, until she met her husband, Ronald, and they married in St Paul's church, Clapham, on this date in 1961. They came to live here in Clanfield, Hampshire, very soon after."

There was more about Rose's activities in and around Clanfield and her reputation as a very intellectual lady who started a book club and read *The Times*. But it was the earlier part of her life, so much at odds with everything the Oxford contingent had been told about it, that caused incredulous astonishment. Ted's group and Valerie's were equally non-plussed. Where was the Rose who had been born and brought up in Spain and was 'totally uneducated' except by an English governess? Ted was of course convinced that Rachel had simply got it all wrong, apart perhaps from the date of the marriage, but was so incensed at her supposedly erroneous version of Rose's life figuring in the service booklet that he managed to refrain from weeping until almost the end of the vicar's address when she stated that Rose had died peacefully in the early hours of the morning and her friend Rachel had been with her. As poor Ted of course considered that *he* should have been the one to stay with Rose in her final hours he began to shed tears both visibly and indeed audibly. Millie kindly put a hand on his arm to comfort him and Emily uttered an indeterminate sound which could have been taken for a giggle. Millie regarded her anxiously, knowing that she was often inclined to give way to inappropriate laughter in awkward or distressing situations. It was certainly to be hoped that this would not add to the embarrassment of the present occasion. Fortunately some music began to be played, not on the organ but a CD. It was from the overture of Puccini's *La Boheme.* This was identified in the Order of Service, though no reason was given for its inclusion. At least it provided a welcome cover for any untoward sounds.

The service progressed with readings from poems, pieces of prose and a few prayers, none of which was familiar or recognisable. They had presumably been composed by the writer of the service booklet. Mary Ann reflected that there was nothing even vaguely reminiscent of the Anglican Book of Common Prayer, and Benedicta and Martha thought it all very Protestant and rather surprising as a memorial for a Catholic. As the congregation progressed to the graveyard for the burial of Rose's ashes beside those of her husband, some rather jolly modern music was played; then there were more prayers and a blessing, which was at least a recognisable item. Ted was still unable to stop shedding tears, but at least managed to do so more quietly, except when he blew his nose. The congregation broke into groups, which progressed to the local pub 'for refreshments' as the invitation in the service booklet bid them.

Rachel somehow managed to be already there when everybody else arrived. She greeted Valerie and her group effusively, even though she had previously done so at the door of the church. When Ted and his group appeared, however, she turned away as if they were simply not there. Inside it was the same. Rachel was very much the grieving next-of-kin in charge of the whole affair and made it her business to speak to all the attending mourners, apart from Ted, Emily, Millie and Marjorie. They were ignored. This was even noticed by the locals, most of whom knew 'Theodore', at least by sight, from his having spent so much time there with Rose. One or two of them made an effort to redress the balance and went to speak to him and meet his companions. There was some hardly hidden surprise when Emily was introduced as his wife.

Mary Ann was embarrassed at the treatment meted out to what was clearly regarded as the opposing group, as she knew them all and did not wish to incur the animosity of any of them, particularly Marjorie. Benedicta spoke of it to Martha, who regarded the whole situation as full of interest.

"I'm going to speak to them," Mary Ann announced. "People should know how to behave."

It was not certain which people she meant and she had no wish to offend Valerie, as after all she had to travel back to Oxford in her car. But she reflected that if Valerie took umbrage she could always say she'd been trying to find out how *they'd* managed to acquire Rose's car. She went over to where 'they' were standing with only one local person speaking to them and placed herself between Emily and Millie.

"You must have had a good trip down," she remarked pleasantly, "you left after us and you were here before us!"

"Oh yes, Ted knows the road well." Emily seemed

quite unabashed at imparting this information.

"I suppose it's a fast car, too," Mary Ann continued.

"It's certainly more comfortable than the old one," Millie volunteered, "especially with four of us in it."

Mary Ann felt she was not getting anywhere fast so she went on. "Has he, I mean," she realised she should be speaking to Emily, "have *you* had it long?"

"Well, only since Rose passed away, of course, it was her car, you see." Emily volunteered no further information about the acquisition of the car and another local person came up to them. Martha also joined them as she had not previously met any of the group apart from Marjorie and was interested in doing so. Bent as she already was on solving the mystery of Rose's conflicting identities she decided that some local reactions might be useful. Having been introduced to Ted, Emily and Millie as Marjorie's new housemate she turned her attention to the local couple, evidently husband and wife, who had joined the group.

"Friends of the deceased, I suppose?" she addressed them.

"Well, we belonged to her book group," the husband answered. "She was very intellectual but she chose books we all enjoyed, I mean like *The Go-between* and, um, *Brideshead* um, what was it, Mary? Oh yes, *Revisited.* Well, you'd seen that on telly, hadn't you? I found it a bit heavy."

"Expect a Cambridge graduate to be intellectual, wouldn't you? Told you about that, did she?"

"She didn't say much about it, did she Mary? Talked about the books, mainly."

"I don't really remember, Arthur. Oh yes, though, she did say it was very cold there. But is that how you knew her? At Cambridge?" The wife politely addressed Martha.

"No; met her at church. Catholic."

"Oh, we're Church of England; well, we go sometimes. I thought Rose was a friend of the lady vicar. P'raps she did go to the Catholic church, though. But there isn't one here. I think Catholics go to Peterborough. Isn't that right, Arthur?"

"I wouldn't know. But Ronald, her husband, he never went to any church. He wasn't keen on that sort of thing at all."

"Devoted couple, though, were they?" Martha was interested to know.

"Well, he didn't come to the book club so we didn't see them together that much. But they used to have people round for coffee in their big kitchen. It was warm in there. They had an Aga. It was a big house to heat for just two people. They talked a lot about the news in the paper. They had *The Times*. Or was it *The Guardian*, Arthur? We take *The Telegraph* ourselves."

Mary and Arthur continued to talk more about themselves than about Rose and her husband and

Martha managed to make Mary Ann listen to them while she paid more attention to the other three. She quickly decided that Millie was very good value and would be a considerable help in her investigations and Millie responded to her interest without either of them needing to explain overtly that they wanted to find out more about the mysteries of Rose's background. Benedicta had reluctantly found it necessary to give in to the needs of her ninety-plus years and sit down, which effectively removed her from general conversation.

People began to drift away. Neither Emily nor Millie had ever met Rachel so they felt it unnecessary to make any effort to approach her. Marjorie considered Rachel's behaviour quite unacceptable and Ted was much too upset to add any extra stress to the situation. Mary Ann was disgusted by what she considered a very vulgar display of animosity and did not join Valerie in bidding their as-it-were hostess goodbye. She had the excuse that she was looking after Benedicta, who was tired, and Martha, who was a new acquaintance. Valerie was greatly tempted to impart to her now friend Rachel the news that, despite all her efforts to prevent it, Theodore was in possession of Rose's car, but other people were too numerous and time was too limited, so this momentous piece of information had to be kept for another occasion.

CHAPTER 17

As Ted's car and Valerie's car journeyed back to Oxford their occupants were similarly engaged in discussing the version of Rose's life as outlined in the service. Ted was adamant in maintaining that it was all nonsense; that Rose had been born and brought up in Spain and had never even been to school, let alone university. Marjorie agreed that Rose had frequently mentioned that she was 'totally uneducated' and had merely had an English governess in Spain. Millie said little but reflected that she had often wondered about the genuineness of Rose's assertions. She had even once suggested to Ted that 'p'raps Rose wasn't being quite straight with him' — only to be met with angry assertions to the contrary. Emily laughed occasionally but said nothing.

In Valerie's car the discussion was more general. Mary Ann was interested in the discrepancy between the description of Rose and Ronald as a most devoted couple and the impression always given by Rose to the inhabitants of number nine that her husband had played so much golf and hence been so absent from her life that she barely remembered him.

"It's not too surprising she never got round to arranging a memorial service for him," Mary Ann remarked, "but then there's all this about *her* service being on the same day as his funeral and her ashes buried in his grave! Not to mention that it all took place on their wedding anniversary!"

Valerie had nothing immediate to say to this as it could only mean that Rachel's view of Rose, and presumably that of other neighbours in Hampshire, must be at odds with the impression deliberately given to Rose's Oxford acquaintances. As Rachel was now her friend and Rose never really had been she was inclined to feel that Rachel must have got it right.

"Well," she finally ventured after some thought, "it can't be that Rachel was making things up; after all, most of the people at the funeral knew Rose when she was living there, married to Ronald. They must have been at his funeral, too."

"What about Girton College Cambridge?" Martha enquired. "Doesn't go with 'totally uneducated'. Easy to find out about that if we can get hold of her maiden name. Born in Birmingham? Thought you all said Spain. Sure she told me Argentina — first time I met her. Told her I knew it well, often went there. Seemed to avoid me after that. Interesting. Good. I'll find out. Give me something to do. Like a mystery. Solved a few working with the charity.

Had to find kids' identity — birth certificates — so they could be recognised as existing, get jobs."

Benedicta, usually loquacious, said nothing. She had fallen asleep.

Martha wasted no time in getting to work on the mystery of Rose's background. She had already learned all there was to know from her house mates and had early decided that the most useful and least biased informant would be Millie Gatward, whom she contacted the following day and drove out to visit. They sat companionably over a large pot of tea and Millie proved to be an even more useful informant than Martha could have hoped for as she had actually been approached by, and had spoken to, Rose's erstwhile flatmate in London, Siobhan O'Halloran, at the memorial service.

"How? When? Go on - all of it!" Martha poised a pen over her note pad and Millie proceeded.

"It was when we were standing by the grave and that music — you know, about dancing somewhere — was playing and we were waiting for the other people and the vicar lady. I'd somehow got separated from our group and of course Ted was very upset and he was standing a bit of a way off with his face in a handkerchief half the time and this lady I didn't know came up to me. So I asked if she was local or a relative and she said no, she was the flatmate mentioned in the service sheet, Siobhan O'Halloran. Then she asked about me and I said I was with friends of Rose's from Oxford, with Ted Habgood and some others. Then she looked, well, *shocked* I s'pose you'd say, but worse than that, um...."

"Appalled?" suggested Martha.

"Yes, that's it," Millie agreed gratefully. "And then she said 'What? Is *he* here?' And I said 'yes, he's over there, look; you can't miss him, he's tall enough.' And she sort of gasped and looked, well, disgusted, and said 'how *dreadful*'. But then the vicar started talking and we couldn't say any more and I didn't manage to see the lady again afterwards and I wouldn't have known what to say if I had, really."

"Marvellous! Fascinating! Told Ted about it, did you?"

"Yes, I did. He came round that night after we'd got back and I told him then. Well, I mean I told him about this lady speaking to me and who she was, you know, Rose's flatmate in London, but I didn't say how she'd been about him. Then he said he was going to contact her and get at the truth. I s'pose he meant the truth about Rose, but I was a bit surprised because I thought he'd always believed what Rose said. Anyway, I thought it would be awful if he did contact this Siobhan O'Halloran because he'd only be upset, the way she went on about him."

"Didn't know her, did he? Never met her at all?" Martha inquired, though the answer was obvious.

"No, he hadn't even heard of her before. And she can't have really known him or she'd have recognised him at the service, wouldn't she? You can't miss him."

"Only *heard* about him, obviously — very bad things at that! Who from, though, eh? Rachel or *Rose herself*? Wonder!!" Martha was intrigued. This was proving more fascinating than she could have hoped for. "Can't you contact her?"

Millie looked a little distressed. "I don't know how to. I don't know where she lives. I — I don't really like to. I told Ted not to."

"Hmph! Maybe I can. Possible. Might contact that Rachel, find out from her. Time enough. Have another look at the outline biography in this Order of Service. Pick out discrepancies. Here's a list." Martha presented some hastily written notes for Millie to read. They were in two columns denoting the differences in what she had headed as the Oxford and the Hampshire versions of Rose's life history.

OXFORD

Born: Spain/Argentina

Education: Only with an English governess 'Almost totally uneducated'.
Pre-marriage work, life etc: never mentioned apart from living in Spain/Argentina.

Golf widow. Husband so frequently absent she hardly noticed when he died. HAMPSHIRE

Born: Birmingham. Education: Girton College Cambridge.

Teaching in girls' schools; one year in Spain exchange teaching.

Flat share in London with Siobhan O'H. Married there; good husband. Very devoted couple.

"There; now what to work on. Girton easy to check. Have to find maiden name. Given date of marriage and church; name in that if accurate. Right. Away to get on with it. Thanks for tea. My place next time. Bye." Martha was up and out and into her car and snorting away with it at full speed almost before Millie had time to get to the front door herself.

"Phew!" said Millie and looked at her watch, hoping it was time for a drink. It was only half past five but she decided to think ahead just a little and pour herself a much needed gin and tonic before she could summon the strength to go over Martha's notes and her own recollections.

Martha, however, arriving back at number nine inspired rather than tired, turned on her computer and googled St Paul's church, Clapham. She found where its records were kept and how to make contact and find out about them and promptly emailed an enquiry about the marriage of Ronald Ellis Thorneycroft on the date given in the Order of Service. She then telephoned Valerie and invited her to come and have a drink. Despite the suddenness of the invitation, which was hardly surprising from Martha, Valerie was pleased to comply. Over large glasses of wine and a packet of crisps she was asked how well she knew Rachel Thompson and could she introduce her to Martha, soon. "Want to find her angle on things," Martha continued. "Does she know how to contact the O'Halloran woman; want to meet her, too. Pre-marriage stuff most controversial. Attitude to husband controversial, too."

"Well, I've been thinking I'd ask Rachel to come and stay with me. We got on really well and I don't want to lose track of her. I'll get you in to meet her if she comes."

"Good. Thanks. Can't do more than that."

"I'm sure you'll find Rachel knows all about Rose," Valerie was determined to put her friend in the right, "though I can't think why it's different here."

"Difference in Rose. Different stories. Different persona. Different reinventions. New place, new story."

"Yes, you're right," Valerie mused thoughtfully, "it's not Rachel's fault what she's been told any more than ours. It's natural to believe what people say about themselves. But something like this — it makes you wonder what's the truth behind it all."

"I'll find out. Set on it. Let you know. Get Rachel here. Should help. More wine? Right. See you tomorrow." With a brisk nod Martha stood up and thus effectively dismissed her guest.

CHAPTER 18

Mary Ann Evans went to church on Sunday as usual and managed to whisper to her friend Clarissa before the service that she would tell her about Rose's strange Memorial Service afterwards when they went for a drink. Before they left the church, however, they spoke to Millie, who had decided to attend that Sunday as Ted had seemed particularly upset in the days following the journey to Hampshire and she wanted to support him as much as possible. While he was in the vestry taking off his cassock and surplice she made a point of speaking to Mary Ann as she was grateful to her for joining the 'Ted group' at the reception in the pub.

"Well, really," said Mary Ann in response to Millie's thanks, "the whole thing was very strange, wasn't it? But Martha's determined to get to the bottom of it. You know her, don't you?"

"I do now; she came to see me and I'm to see her again this week. She's hoping to have some news."

"What's this?" Clarissa chimed in. "What you said you'd tell me over a drink, is it? I'm intrigued."

Millie saw Ted emerge from the vestry and murmured that she'd better go and Clarissa and Mary Ann decamped to the Royal Oak, where the Memorial Order of Service was mulled over and the strange discrepancies discussed.

"Well, I've heard about people who reinvent themselves totally and people who tell different stories to everybody they meet, but this seems like two separate sets of fiction, each fairly steadily maintained. You really do want to find out not only *what* the person's made up but *why* they should have done so. Poor Millie looked quite disturbed by it and she's usually such a cheerful, matter-of-fact sort of person."

"I'm not surprised she's upset," Mary Ann agreed. "It's very hard to distinguish what actually *is* fact in all this. It can't be pleasant to know that somebody you thought of as a friend was telling you lies all the time. And then the way she and Ted and the other two were treated by that Rachel at the church and the reception was quite shameful. I've never seen such a vulgar display of animosity!"

"Ted looks even thinner and more unhappy than ever, too," Clarissa commented. "Not that he's exactly one of my favourite people, nor I one of his, but he is a member of my choir and I can't help feeling he's been badly treated and he's certainly suffering. I really would like to hear the truth about that woman who died, too. An unsolved mystery's always frustrating."

"I'll certainly let you know if Martha finds anything out, and I'm sure she will," Mary Ann promised. "She's like a hound following a scent and just about as energetic."

Mary Ann's prediction was not far wrong but the first person Martha informed of her findings was Millie, who went to have tea with her a few days later.

"Found something jolly interesting," was Martha's only preamble. "Married in St Paul's church, Clapham, on the very day given, Ronald Ellis Thorneycroft and Rose Mary Amelia Simpson. Tell me there could have been another man of that name married in that church on that day — impossible! Even in London. Got to be Rose's real name: Simpson. Not very Spanish!"

"Now that certainly is interesting," Millie agreed. "And I did ask Ted what he'd been told was Rose's maiden name and he wrote it down. It does look Spanish. Here, can you read it?"

Martha took the proffered piece of paper from Millie and laughed as she read what was on it. "Siramosa! Ha ha ha! See what she's done? Taken the first two letters of her surname — S and i — and jumbled in another two from it, an m and an o, and a couple of As, and here's a Spanish sounding name. Load of guff! No more Spanish than I am. Not even a Catholic, either. Looked up that St Paul's church: middle-of-the-road C of E. Didn't have to get married there because the husband wanted it; we know he was an atheist — big point made of it.

A Catholic who marries outside the church is ex-communicated; very serious."

"I always thought they'd been married in a registry office," Millie murmured. "I'm sure that's what I'd been told. I didn't know about the ex - ex…"

"Excommunication! No; sounds as if *she* didn't know about it either! Must have talked to Hampshire people about the church they were married in; could hardly lie about it in the husband's hearing. No wedding pictures anywhere, I s'pose."

"No," Millie replied musingly. "There were no photographs at all, anywhere. And I remember once when we were all at the service by the big old roundabout, you know, the one with the organ, before the St Giles' Fair, when Ted's church choir was there all dressed up and the local newspaper photographers wanted to take photographs, she got very stroppy with them and put her hands up in front of her face and turned round."

"That figures. Look at the Order of Service."

"Yes, you're right. I've been to lots and lots of funerals and they all had Orders of Service with at least one photo of the deceased; sometimes one on the front, like when the person was old, and another on the back of when they were young. But hers only has that picture of a rose on the front. I s'pose that was Rachel's idea."

"Couldn't use a photo if there weren't any. Now, the Girton College Cambridge thing. Contacted them; they're looking into it. No definite reply yet. Let you know when there is."

Millie expressed her gratitude for the tea and the information and went to catch her bus home. She was so deep in thought on the journey that she missed her stop and had to walk back from the next one. She was mainly wondering how much to tell Ted about Martha's findings. He had expressed a wish to find out the truth from Siobhan O'Halloran, but Millie was not at all sure that he really wanted to know it. He knew Rose had not given accurate information about her age, but that was hardly unusual or surprising in a woman of her generation and as he'd always put it: "Rose didn't tell lies, exactly, she just let you guess things and didn't say if you'd got it wrong." This would, however, hardly cover the invention of a Spanish name and origin and a schoolless upbringing with a governess in a foreign country. Millie decided to say nothing at least for the moment, but she had to admit to herself that she was finding it less and less easy to tolerate Ted's emotional outpourings over Rose's death. She felt she had little choice in the matter as he kept insisting that she was 'the only person he could talk to about it'. He had, however, invited her to a dinner in his college the following week and she hoped he might be in a slightly more normal state by then and at least manage to eat something.

Mary Ann managed to glean information from Martha in advance of her next meeting at and after church with her friend Clarissa, whom she had promised to keep informed of any developments. By that time Martha had heard from Girton College and was able to produce a copy of the email she had received from that source. She showed it to Mary Ann as they sat over an early evening glass of wine. Mary Ann's ex-husband provided her with the wherewithal to keep quite a good cellar. She read with interest:

Dear Mrs Prout,

I apologise for my delay in responding to your recent enquiry to track down Rose M.A.Thorneycroft. I have checked the College records and also checked with our Archivist and, unfortunately, we have no record of a Rose Thorneycroft née Simpson coming to Girton. I am sorry that we are unable to help you and good luck with your search.

Kind regards,

etc, etc.

"Well well," Mary Ann commented, "that certainly settles that. Of course it was only a Hampshire story, not an Oxford one."

"Knew she couldn't get away with it in Oxford so went to the other extreme: 'entirely uneducated'! Clever! Knew what she was about."

"You're certainly right there," Mary Ann agreed. "And it might sound very special in a Hampshire village for a woman of that generation to have been to Cambridge, but in Oxford it's in no way remarkable. It's very much more special and interesting to be something exotic, and decidedly unusual - and upmarket - to be governess educated."

"Too many Cambridge graduates in Oxford, too," Martha commented. "Might ask awkward questions. Ignorance about the place soon shown up."

"It was a bit of a risk pretending to be Spanish, though," Mary Ann mused, "even if it was true that she'd been there for a year as an exchange teacher and knew the language. She can't have spoken perfect Spanish with no English accent."

"Hmph! Argentina she told me. Same language of course. Kept to friends who were not linguists. Talked a lot about other things. Good talker, wasn't she?"

"Yes, she was; very lively really and talked about things she'd just been doing. Quite a good listener, too - she did show interest in other people. I think we all liked her." Mary Ann spoke with something like surprise. Somehow she had come to feel that the Rose they were discussing was not the same person that they had known when she was living in the house with them. "It's very strange," she murmured, "I'd almost begun to feel as if she didn't really exist."

"Didn't, in a way," was Martha's brief comment. "Even pretended to be a Catholic, which she wasn't at all."

"No, really? Are you sure? Why should anybody do that?"

Martha outlined her discoveries about the church in which the marriage took place and Rose's failure to attend any masses apart from a very occasional one at Blackfriars with Benedicta. "Didn't even go at Easter."

"Well," Mary Ann admitted, "I used not to go much, though I'd have always said I was an Anglican. Not that anybody asked me. I've only been going lately because I've made friends at the church, well, one particular friend, and found it really very interesting altogether. Several titled people go there, you know. But nobody ever asked if I was an Anglican. I could have been a Methodist or nothing at all."

"Hmph! Doesn't work like that for Catholics." Martha was dismissive of Protestant practices, though she was not unfamiliar with them. "Not in England, anyway. Can't just join up by going along; can't receive the sacraments. Big thing, being a Catholic — even a not very good Catholic. Can't receive Holy Communion without being in a state of grace — terrible sin."

"Oh dear! What's a state of grace?" Mary Ann had never heard the term.

"Hard to explain. Being cut off from God because of sin means you're *not* in a state of grace. Even missing Mass on Sunday's enough for that to happen."

"Well, I do think that's very over strict. How long do people stay cut off like that?" Mary Ann was slightly incredulous.

"Until they've been to confession and been absolved by a priest. See what it means just not bothering to go to Mass, then? Anybody who calls themselves a Catholic knows that. Sounds as if this Rose woman knew very little about being a Catholic. Probably knew the drill; seems to have spent a year in a Catholic country. Might have gone to the odd Mass with a Catholic flatmate — a 'Siobhan O'Halloran' has to be Irish; surely Catholic — knew how to make the sign of the cross if nothing else. Had to make out she was Catholic to go with the Spanish origin, didn't she? Far more interesting than C of E!"

"Yes, you're right," Mary Ann agreed. "It was all part of the exotic persona. But I'm a little surprised Benedicta didn't realise."

"Not something they talked about; Benedicta talks all the time herself. Hard to get a word in edgeways sometimes. Clever though, Benedicta. Mustn't underestimate. Yes, you're right. Surprising. Taken in like everybody else. Don't expect people to tell lies about themselves, do we?"

Mary Ann agreed that we didn't. She felt a slight qualm about the claims to aristocratic connections so often aired by her mother, but considered that slight exaggerations about one's family were hardly in the same category as downright inventions about oneself!

CHAPTER 19

Millie was not greatly enjoying the dinner in Ted's college. The porter had greeted her with a wink and a comment that she might expect more invitations to college meals as things were now and Ted had responded by saying things were certainly sadly different and inviting sympathy by putting his head on the porter's shoulder. "Think of the good times, Ted," was the cheerful response as he deftly removed his shoulder. Not only was Millie embarrassed by this display she was also sadly aware that far from being the only person Ted could talk to about his dire distress at Rose's death, she doubtless shared that supposed distinction with anybody and everybody in his college. This was made even clearer when they met one of the women from the college office, who immediately patted Ted's arm sympathetically and enquired in tones of deep compassion, "How *are* you now, Ted?"

Ted wiped his tear-filled eyes and said chokingly "Well, you know, not any better really."

"Don't try to rush it," the kind woman continued. "Remember what I told you, it took me two years to get over it when my mother died." Ted agreed that he wouldn't try to rush it and Millie, looking on, considered that he was certainly doing very much the reverse. She couldn't help feeling, at the same time, a hint of amusement as she reflected how Rose might have felt about being equated with somebody's mother!

The rest of the evening was of a piece. Ted made something of a parade of his inability to eat more than a few mouthfuls of food and his unwillingness to drink any wine. Millie tried to talk to the person on her other side, but in a graduate college where there is no high table and younger members sit jumbled in with the dons and their guests there is not always a very suitable mix and Millie was unlucky enough to be next to a young man who had clearly come into dinner with a new girlfriend, to whom he was giving all his attention. The people opposite were similarly absorbed with each other and even had they not been, the noise in the rather bare, modern hall with its inadequately high ceiling was not very conducive to conversation with anybody more than eighteen inches away. Millie sighed and hoped they'd at least be able to leave early.

They did in fact leave directly after the meal without waiting for coffee in the Common Room and were back at Millie's house just after nine o'clock. Ted of course opened the front door with his key and went in as he was used to doing. Millie announced that *she* was going to have a cup of tea even if he wasn't and went to put the kettle on. Ted insisted on making the tea though he protested that he didn't want any himself, but Millie fetched another cup, poured generously milked and sugared tea for him and set it down in front of him.

"You've got to stop being like this," she said. "It's gone on long enough. It's not even real. Rose was never straight with you. She told you nothing but lies about herself. She wasn't Spanish at all. She was plain Rose Simpson. She wasn't even a Catholic. That was all part of the Spain fiction. If she was ever there it was only doing a year being an exchange teacher like it said in the Order of Service."

"That's not true! That Rachel made it up. Rose showed me on the internet the house she was born in."

"The house she stayed in when she was an exchange teacher, more like! Come to that, any house she found on the web and took a fancy to! I could show you a picture of a posh house anywhere and say I was born there! And don't go on as if Rose was the great one and only love of your life, either. What about that Bee you were all over all the time she was here? It's not as if you didn't know Rose at the same time!"

Ted stood up and shouted "Why bring that up? Don't talk about Bee. I never loved Bee. Shut up about it. I loved Rose. Rose loved me. I know she did. She told me she did."

"That was a fiction too. It was all pretence and that's why you're wallowing in it like this, because that's how you're trying to make it real."

Ted gave no answer but stormed out of the room and out of the house, slamming the door violently behind him. Millie sat sipping her cup of tea and feeling angry with herself. She should never have given way so and gone on like that, it was all useless and only made things worse. Ted would never believe he was deliberately making himself suffer over an unreality. He'd just have to get over it in his own time, if he wasn't to have a complete breakdown. Millie sighed sadly and reflected how strange it was that Rose, who had seemed to get on well with everybody when she was alive, should be the cause of so much strife and bitterness now that she was dead.

When Rachel Thompson came to stay with Valerie for a few days Martha Prout managed to engineer an invitation to meet her over a cup of coffee. The conversation was easily brought round to Rachel's memories of Rose as she professed herself deeply affected by the loss of her friend and very willing to talk about her.

"Oh yes, I knew her so well, and especially after Ronnie died — Ronnie, that's her husband, Ronald

— of course I saw even more of her then. We were such friends. Oh yes, she was devoted to Ronnie. After he died she put a big picture of him on a table by his chair; I mean the sitting-room chair he always sat in, you know, and from then on nobody ever sat in that chair. It meant so much to Rose."

"Must have brought it here with her, then!" Martha made it a statement rather than a query. "Seen it here, have you?"

Rachel, who had been smiling a soulful smile, suddenly changed her expression for a slightly puzzled frown of concentration. "Well," she said slowly, "I don't think — well I mean — it was different here. I don't think she can have brought it."

"Lots of photos of her husband here, though, were there?" Martha knew the answer but wanted Rachel to have to admit to the total absence of any such photographs.

Valerie was beginning to see that Rachel was not only puzzled but confused and decided to clarify matters. "Well I know I never saw any. She didn't talk about her husband." Valerie was torn between regarding Rachel as a friend and having been no very great fan of Rose. She was also, therefore, very tempted to mention Rose's opening remark at her first encounter with her housemates — 'My husband played rather a lot of golf; I really don't remember when he died' — but decided that Rachel might find such a revelation incredibly shocking, or perhaps shockingly incredible. She looked at Martha, knowing that she had already heard the story, and saw a smile of considerable satisfaction.

Rachel recovered sufficiently to speak. "I suppose when she moved here Rose decided to start a new life free from sad memories."

"Had a new man to look after her too, didn't she?" Martha was less inhibited than Valerie and less inclined to consider Rachel's feelings.

"Oh! You mean that awful Theodore Habgood! She didn't want him. He forced himself on her. Never left her alone. She couldn't get rid of him. He put his nose into everything; tried to control her life."

Even Valerie, averse though she was to 'that Theodore', had to admit that it hadn't quite looked like that. She'd seen Rose walking along arm in arm with Theodore in a most friendly, not to say intimate, fashion; she'd seen the shelves he'd made for her, the pictures he'd put up, the clock he'd restored, the help he'd given at a drinks party. She mused silently and let Martha do the answering.

"Poor woman. Terrible for her. Easily dominated, was she? Not able to stand up for herself? Any man could walk all over her!"

Rachel had to admit to herself that this was hardly a valid assessment of Rose; in fact such a description had nothing of Rose in it at all. But she hastily concentrated on Rose's last days in the hospital when she had banned Theodore from coming to see her and even asked for help in doing so. She managed to agree with Martha's supposed assumptions, unaware that they were actually tongue in cheek. "Yes, it really was like that."

Valerie changed the subject and Martha took her leave and went back to her flat to write up all she had heard and learned so far. Rachel and Valerie went out for a drive in the country and both were careful to avoid the subject of Rose as it was silently understood that they felt rather differently about her.

Ted spent a miserable morning. He had done more weeping than sleeping during the night and was later than usual taking the invariable cup of tea up to his wife. He was not greatly given to introspection and was really unaware of what it was he'd been weeping over. He was angry with Millie and in no way inclined to feel apologetic for his behaviour to her, but he realised he could hardly go round and see her as he usually did before finally setting off for his office in Oxford. He put down his particular sadness to what he considered to be Millie's unkindness to him, combined of course with his continued (and he supposed everlasting) misery over Rose's death. That it was in any way related to any doubts about Rose's integrity, to the truth of any of her statements or her real feelings for him, was something that never occurred to him. His suppression of these doubts never surfaced to his conscious mind, but it was making him ill nevertheless. He could think of nothing but Rose and it made him cry. He wanted to talk about her rather than merely think; thinking alone was something to be avoided. It might lead to questions he did not want to ask himself. He couldn't talk to his wife. He hadn't been able to talk to her for years about anything other than mundane practicalities. Now he couldn't talk to Millie. He'd go and talk to Marjorie; Marjorie had appreciated Rose. She wouldn't say unkind things. She'd understand how he felt. He set off in the car which had belonged to Rose, went to the house where he had seen her so often, drove into the car park and into Valerie's parking space as he had always done. As he went up the familiar back stairs which led to both the flat Rose had inhabited and the one on the top floor belonging to Marjorie he wept more and more copiously. By the time he knocked on the door he was barely in a state to speak. Marjorie was not merely astonished to see him but quite aghast at his appearance.

"Ted! Whatever's the matter?" she exclaimed. The only answer was a sob as Ted followed her into the room on to which the door opened directly. "Sit down. What can I get you? A drink? Brandy?" Ted shook his head and continued to weep for some minutes until he finally blew his nose. Marjorie had directed plays and was a devotee of drama. Sorry though she was for Ted and genuinely moved by his obvious misery, she was unable to suppress a quite objective perception of the almost comic effect of the fog-horn like noise he made. If that were to happen on a stage, she reflected, the audience would certainly laugh. She thrust a small glass of brandy into his hand and told him to drink it.

"What is it?" he demanded. "I don't drink now."

"Medicine," said Marjorie, "cough mixture." She had indeed used it as such when giving a lecture or doing a reading. She'd always found it most effective against dry throats and coughs.

Ted took a small, suspicious sip. "I stopped drinking when Rose was ill. Stopped smoking too. I thought if I did God might let her live. She always wanted me to stop smoking. She said 'I don't want you dying before I do'." At this memory Ted broke down again and Marjorie took the brandy from his hand as he was in danger of spilling it.

"Well, at least that hasn't happened; you should think of it that way and take comfort from it," Marjorie said kindly.

"I can't take comfort from anything. I look at people in the street, old people. They look much older than Rose and I hate them for being alive when she isn't. It's not fair. She shouldn't have died. They got it all wrong at the hospital. She had so much to live for."

Marjorie became aware of a movement at the door of the room, which Ted had not closed as he came in. It was Martha Prout.

"Oh, heavens! Martha! I'm so sorry — you're coming for a drink — oh dear I'd forgotten, well not exactly, I mean..."

"No, no. Obviously busy. Not your fault. Door was open; didn't want to interrupt; just to tell you *I* hadn't forgotten. Another time." Martha returned to her own flat and happily added to the notes she'd already made concerning her encounter with Valerie and Rachel. She had, she considered, spent a particularly satisfactory morning.

CHAPTER 20

Mary Ann regaled her friend-at-church Clarissa with 'the story so far' regarding the mystery of Rose. They observed that Ted was looking more thin, worn and sorrowful with each Sunday and that he hardly spoke to anybody and never stayed after services to have a drink. Martha had let Mary Ann know that she had some news to impart and Mary Ann invited her to impart it over a 'proper' tea, to which she also invited Millie and Clarissa. They sat at the dining table and regarded with considerable anticipatory satisfaction the sandwiches, scones and cakes taking up most of its surface.

As a preamble Mary Ann introduced the topic of what to call such a spread these days. "When I was young it was absolutely normal to have this sort of thing every day and it was always called 'tea'. And there were tearooms and this was what you expected to have in such places. Now they seem to want to call it 'high tea'. I used to think 'high tea' was a kind of evening meal, like a sort of early dinner."

"I've never heard anybody actually talking about

having 'high tea'," Clarissa volunteered, "people who made it their evening meal just called it 'tea' and only people who despised them called it 'high tea'. It's terrible the way meals have got different names and are eaten at different times in England; it doesn't happen in other countries."

"Oh, you're absolutely right; it's so confusing," Mary Ann agreed. "I had a maid — er, I mean a help — once and if people rang and asked for me in the morning when I was out she'd tell them I'd be back 'after dinner'. Of course she meant dinner at twelve o'clock and that I'd be back in the afternoon; but my callers would ring back late in the evening because they'd know I had dinner at seven or eight! So tiresome!"

"What about 'afternoon tea'?" Millie enquired. "Isn't this what we're having? I mean, what some people call it?"

"Oh dear, yes. 'Beg pardon I'm soiling the doyleys / With afternoon tea cakes and scones'" Mary Ann quoted Betjeman's satirical poem *How to get on in Society.* Millie looked puzzled and Martha felt that the name of the repast they were enjoying had 'nothing to do with the case' and that they were gathered to enjoy it while discussing the question of Rose, or at least some answers to the many questions about her.

"Managed to meet Rachel Thompson," she announced. "Briefly. Coffee with Valerie. Interesting. Very. First big discrepancy: devoted wife. So revered her husband she wouldn't let anybody sit in his chair after he died. Big picture of him sitting in it. In the house in Hampshire. Here in Oxford: no chair; no pictures. Said she saw him so little she couldn't remember when he died! Implied she didn't notice! *Very* different."

"Yes, that's absolutely what happened here; I well remember it. We were all — well — not exactly shocked, but taken aback, though I could sympathise." Mary Ann's ex-husband had not yet died but she would not have noticed much, if any, difference if he had.

"Well I *am* surprised!" Millie looked as shocked as Rose's flatmates had originally been. "I've never heard about that before. She sometimes talked to us about her husband, Ronnie she called him, and about things he'd done for her like designing a beautiful kitchen. She seemed a bit upset because the people who bought her house had it all taken out."

"Oh, isn't it dreadful!" Mary Ann pounced on her favourite bone of contention "That's what happens all the time in these big expensive houses; the whole neighbourhood's made to look like a perpetual building site because the new owners tear everything out and replace it. Then they only live in it for a couple of years before they sell the house and the next owners do the same thing!"

"Talked to you about her husband, did she?" Martha responded to Millie, ignoring Mary Ann. "Ted there too, I suppose."

"Oh yes, he usually was. Of course he'd known Rose for a long time in Hampshire and stayed in the house there and all."

"Different story about her husband to him, then. Neglectful golfer story wouldn't wash. Didn't say it in front of him, did she!"

Mary Ann agreed that she didn't and Clarissa, puzzled, asked why ever she should have said such a thing at all!

"Obvious." Martha pronounced. "Didn't want questions asked here about her marriage, where it was, when, what church. Spoil the 'Spanish Catholic' pretence."

"Ted thinks she was a Spanish Catholic, though," Millie objected. "But I'm sure he said she'd been married in a registry office. He thinks she lived in Spain till she came to England and got married — but he did say she never much wanted to talk about it because living in Spain under Franco was so terrible and she'd rather forget it. I tried to tell him she wasn't being straight with him, that he couldn't trust what she said, but he flung out in a rage and I haven't seen him for a few days now. I thought he might be less miserable if he could face the truth, know she wasn't all she said she was. But now he's worse if anything. I feel awful about it."

"Needn't. He should know he's wrong. Languishing over a chimaera!" Martha had no patience with such wilful self delusion.

Millie was puzzled. "A camera?" she enquired.

Mary Ann hastened to explain. She'd actually thought of the word in the course of her ponderings on Rose some days earlier and had looked it up to make sure she'd got it right. She was never averse to airing her knowledge of foreign languages. "No, a ky-meera." She pronounced the word more strongly than Martha had. "A fantasy, a delusion."

"Oh. Yes. Sometimes I think he does know that, but he can't bear to lose hold of it," Millie ventured.

"I believe you're right." Clarissa was interested. "He deliberately keeps himself in such a state because he thinks — subconsciously, of course — that if he stays in the depths of distress the cause of it must be real."

"How must his wife feel about his behaving like this over another woman?" Mary Ann enquired. "Surely embarrassed, if nothing else."

"Well, we don't see so much of it at church, do we?" Clarissa commented. "He comes late and leaves early these days. The way he went on over that Bee woman must have been — was — more embarrassing."

"It's really bad in his college, though," Millie averred. "He talks about it all the time to everyone. But Emily's not there very often. There's no knowing how she feels; she never talks about it.

She never looks or sounds any different."

"Only other thing to know about, that Siobhan O'Halloran. Why so shocked Ted was at the service? Hm?" Martha looked at Millie, who outlined briefly to the others her encounter with Rose's London flat mate.

"Pity you didn't get more out of her. See if I can track her down. Whole story then, marriage and all."

"The one thing nobody can really get hold of though," Clarissa observed thoughtfully, "is Rose's motivation. Why should she want to reinvent herself? What did she achieve by it?"

"That's probably a matter for a psychiatrist," Mary Ann answered, "and it's just a trifle late for Rose to consult one! Not that I can imagine she ever would have. She must have enjoyed presenting her various *personae* to different people. Isn't it called the Walter Mitty syndrome?"

"I don't think it matters why she did it," Millie said sadly, "it's more what it's done to other people that matters now, because it's still happening. I wake up in the night sometimes and it comes into my head and won't go away. Ted's having something like a breakdown over it and Marjorie's very unhappy because she's spoken up for Ted and she feels everybody here's against her."

"You're absolutely right," Mary Ann agreed, "and it used not to be like this. Rose wanted to convince each and everyone she felt safe with that they and only they were her very best and most particular friend. When she first came she called herself by a different variant of the name 'Rose' to each of us, all geared to what she thought would most appeal to that person — calling herself 'Rosario' to a religious woman like Benedicta, for example."

"Whatever else she was, she must have been very clever," Clarissa observed.

"Ted keeps saying she was the cleverest woman he's ever known," said Millie, "though that was mainly because he taught her to do sudokus and she caught on really fast. But he did say she was even worse than me with a computer; only he seems to have forgotten about that."

Clarissa laughed "She must have been very much cleverer than he is, anyway. How many people could sum up women they hardly knew well enough to know what variant of a name would appeal to them? Or, come to that, be able to maintain different stories about themselves so successfully that the disparity was only perceived when the different people went to the Memorial Service?"

"Not to mention that she passed herself off as ten or twelve years younger than she really was," Mary Ann spoke feelingly. "One really does have to admire that!"

There was general laughter and the tea finished on a lighter note than might have been anticipated at its beginning. Martha, however, felt that the mystery of Rose was still insufficiently solved and she firmly intended to contact Siobhan O'Halloran by any means possible.

CHAPTER 21

Mary Ann was inclined to regard the tea she had organised and provided as a successful social occasion but she had been struck by Millie's observation that Marjorie was unhappy at the apparent enmity of her house mates and she did have to admit to feeling a little guilty on that score herself. She pondered on the means of improving matters. Her last invitation to Marjorie had gone decidedly awry, so another one would probably not be gratefully received. She decided instead to take Marjorie some flowers or a flowering plant as a peace offering and combine it with a carefully worded apology. Acting on this the following day she climbed the rather numerous stairs from her '*piano nobile*' to Marjorie's top floor, feeling glad she had chosen a bunch of flowers rather than a heavy pot plant, and knocked on the door. It was opened with some delay — Marjorie did not move with ease or speed — and ensuing astonishment.

"Heavens!" was Marjorie's immediate response. Mary Ann did not indicate any intention to enter the room but merely offered the flowers saying:

"I'm so sorry to have offended you, Marjorie. It really is too awfully distressing. I hope you'll accept this tiny offering. Please say you will."

Marjorie took the bouquet with a graceful gesture of her right hand, wiped her brow with an equally eloquent sweep of the back of her left hand and gave a pained and patient smile. "Oh, of *course, do* come in!" she said, and Mary Ann followed her inside.

"*Do* sit down. I'll just put these lovely flowers in water." Marjorie disappeared into the kitchen and took some little time before she returned with the flowers in a vase. She then sat down opposite her visitor and waited for her to speak.

There was a silence as Mary Ann searched for some variant of what she had already said. Finally she managed. "It's so sad, Marjorie, the way we're all at odds. When Rose was here she seemed to get on with everybody and we all got on with one another — well, most of the time. And now we're all taking sides and you're unhappy with Benedicta and with me and Valerie's unhappy with you; and that poor fellow who, whatever his faults — after all, he can't help — well, he used to be very kind and helpful to all of us, seems to be having a breakdown; oh dear!" Mary Ann had felt she must put in a good word for Ted/Theodore as contention over him was rather a key issue and the principal cause of her own offending of Marjorie, but the combination of so many ideas into one utterance was more than she could cope with and she gave up the unequal struggle and decided to wipe her eyes in a gesture more eloquent than speech.

Marjorie responded with a heavy sigh. "Ah, yes, how true. I do feel that Benedicta was quite out of order to interfere. *I* should have arranged for a clergyman to see Rose; *I* was her most particular friend here..."

Marjorie broke off with a sob and Mary Ann hastily responded. "Oh, did you know Rose wasn't actually a Catholic?"

"Oh, wasn't she? Does it matter?"

"I'm sure Benedicta thinks so. Catholics are very particular about it; many of them have died for their faith." An Anglican nurtured in an Anglo-Catholic school, Mary Ann did have some notion of the importance of adherence to one's faith.

"Oh, yes, of course, so did some Protestants; but that was *hundreds* of years ago when they thought they'd go to hell if they died with the wrong label. Surely that doesn't matter *now!*" Marjorie was not impressed with Benedicta's possible opinion on the subject.

"Haven't you read *Brideshead Revisited?*" Mary Ann was genuinely surprised at Marjorie's attitude. "The girl in that wouldn't marry a divorced man because she couldn't be a Catholic if she did — and there's a most affecting scene of her father finally dying a Catholic!"

"Oh, fiction! Very good drama, of course, but how many people could really take it seriously? Though I do know it was a book Rose was keen on. I've always thought it rather over-rated, myself."

Mary Ann decided to let the subject drop; she had no wish to mar her peace mission and felt it advisable to say only that somebody of Benedicta's age, especially one who'd been a nun, might feel such things more strongly. Marjorie at least conceded a 'well, perhaps...' and Mary Ann seized the moment, more concerned with placating Marjorie than with strict adherence to veracity. "After all, you know, it was most likely to have been Rachel who asked Benedicta to see about getting a priest, not Benedicta who initiated it."

The effect on Marjorie was startling. No longer languid and wearily patient she sat up and almost shouted. "So that's it! I might have realised! That Rachel — she's behind everything! All the friction's due to her; look how she behaved about Rose's car: selling it for scrap rather than getting a decent price for it from Ted! The spite of the woman! I hope she knows he's got it now. You know I actually had to leave a class and drive him up to the garage to buy it because he was so terrified Rachel would somehow manage to thwart him?"

Mary Ann was all attention. "No! Really? I didn't know how he'd got it. When was this?"

"Oh, you must remember. He left his old car

here because he came banging on my door saying 'Please! You must help me! I must go and get Rose's car before Rachel stops me!' Of course she couldn't have stopped him; she wasn't even here or anywhere in Oxford, but he was quite beside himself and I had to leave my class and let him drive to the garage in my car so that he could rush in there and buy Rose's. He just left me sitting in my car and I had the most *awful* time driving back to Oxford in the dark and then when I had finally arrived home he rang and made me promise not to let anybody know about it in case Rachel came and took it from him! I tried to tell him he was being completely paranoid, but it was no use, I had to promise. It shows what sort of state he was in."

"Oh dear, how absolutely dreadful! It must have been most upsetting for you. And you couldn't even confide in anybody. I *do* feel for you!" Mary Ann in fact felt distinctly guilty and ashamed of the suspicions she had harboured — and conveyed to others — about the reason for the overnight stay of Ted's old car in number nine's car park. She consoled herself swiftly by agreeing wholeheartedly that it was all due to the malice of Rachel. "And you're *entirely* right!" she averred fervently, "that Rachel has a vast amount to answer for!"

Marjorie sat back in her chair, quite wrung out by her vivid reminiscence, and looking decidedly ill. Mary Ann was so alarmed as to say "I think you need a drink. I'll get you something; what would you like? Whisky, brandy, gin?"

Marjorie managed a faint smile and said "Brandy, I think; thank you, most kind."

Mary Ann hastened to her own flat and returned with a bottle of her best brandy. She found glasses in Marjorie's kitchen, poured generous drinks, which they both sipped gratefully, restored to a modicum of peaceful companionship by their mutual antipathy to Rachel.

Martha Prout, meanwhile, was working on the means of contacting Siobhan O'Halloran. She achieved this eventually via Valerie and Rachel, to both of whom she was a neutral participant as she could hardly be accused of any kindly feelings towards Ted/ Theodore, whom she knew only by repute and a brief sighting at the Memorial Service in Hampshire. Reflecting to herself that she could hardly consider Rose's former flatmate as a bull whose horns should be taken, she switched to thinking of her more appropriately as a nettle, probably most suitably grasped with gloves. Accordingly she wrote a letter to send to the address in Clapham supplied by Rachel. Her written style was less abrupt than her usual mode of speech and after some careful consideration she produced the following:

Dear Ms O'Halloran,

I saw you in the distance at the Memorial Service we both attended in Hampshire and enquired about you with interest; my friend Millie Gatward was fortunate enough to meet you in person and I have subsequently heard a great deal about you from Rachel Thompson. I think we might find we have quite a lot in common and I am particularly interested to talk to you as I am writing a small piece about the late Rose Thorneycroft and would very much value your help in filling in some details. I'm coming up to London next week or the week after and if you could possibly spare the time for me to come and see you I would be most extremely grateful.

Yours very sincerely,
(Mrs) Martha Prout.

Having duly considered the contents of her missive and decided they were as good as she could manage Martha slipped it into an envelope, along with a card giving her own details and email address, rather cursed the fact that she would have to go and buy a stamp, as she hardly used such things these days, duly did so and put the letter in the post box along with a swift prayer for a favourable response.

The response was not very long in coming and was indeed favourable. Although it was a letter, rather than an email as Martha had hoped it might be, it did at least provide a telephone number and suggest a couple of possible dates in the following week. Ms O'Halloran also implied that she would be pleased to talk to 'an interested party' about Rose as she had been accustomed to telephone her from time to time and now missed this contact sadly. Martha duly rang the given number and arranged to visit the house in Clapham on the first of the suggested dates and they had a short but pleasant conversation in which Martha reiterated her interest and Siobhan O'Halloran her willingness to indulge it. So the ancient, green Morris Minor leapt from the drive of number nine on the appointed day and somehow achieved its journey to London, its indicators flicking out as it — amazingly — passed other vehicles or veered off roundabouts or achieved other feats at a speed of which it, and its driver, might have seemed hardly capable. It arrived at the terraced house in Clapham in very good time for the appointed visit over tea.

"Ms O'Halloran? Nice to see you properly. Awfully good of you. Martha Prout. Thank you," was Martha's response to the 'Do come in' of the small, slight woman who opened the door. She was then ushered into the 'front room', which was clearly the main room of the house.

"Nice house. Shared it with Rose, did you?" Martha inquired as she sat in the proffered arm chair.

"Oh no; though we did share a flat in a house near here; a similar sort of house. I only have the ground floor here. We had the top floor in the other house and there was a sitting room and two bedrooms, but the bedrooms were a bit smaller. And there was a kitchen with a bath in it."

"Very typical in the 50s and 60s," Martha commented, "different now, usually. Even in London. Prices terrible. Bad in Oxford, too. Rose with you a long time, was she?"

"Oh yes; really some years. I don't remember exactly how many, but it must have been five or six altogether. She was teaching at a girls' school, you see, well apart from the year she spent in Spain. I was in the office in another school."

"Whole year in Spain, was she?"

"Well, you know, a whole academic year."

"Spoke Spanish, did she?"

"Well she did when she came back. And she'd done classes on it and even a summer course in Cambridge."

"Not a Cambridge graduate, though?"

"Oh, no; she went to a Training College in Birmingham. But I'll bring in the tea."

Siobhan O'Halloran went from the room and Martha noticed that she moved rapidly and with apparent energy and was slightly bow-legged, and concluded that she must be considerably younger than her one time flat mate, whose academic career thus outlined was in fact no news to Martha. She reflected on it lightly as she looked round the room, which was furnished with some comfort and little elegance. Of most interest to the observer were a crucifix on the wall and a statue of the Sacred Heart on the mantlepiece.

In a very short time the tea was wheeled in on a wooden trolley, whose two shelves were bedecked with embroidered cloths under their burden of teapot, china cups and saucers, plates of cakes and biscuits. Martha commented with great appreciation not only on the feast but on the presentation of it.

"Wonderful! Love to see nice china; cups and saucers, too! Sick of mugs - never know where to put them down. Cloths on the trolley; stop things slipping; sensible *and* attractive. Woman after my own heart; see that!"

Her hostess warmed under the praise bestowed and happily furnished an account of her acquisition of the appreciated objects from her mother. "I was the only girl, you see; I had five brothers — well, I've still got four — but I was the only girl, and the second eldest of all. So I had my work cut out helping my mother. How do you like your tea?" Siobhan wielded the large pot, which was clad in a carefully worked tea-cosy. "Strong I hope!" Martha agreed that a good strong cup of tea was entirely desirable. "Glad I am to hear that," her hostess beamed as she poured the dark brown liquid, "like my mother used to say: 'none of your shamrock tea here!'"

"Shamrock tea?" Martha was aware that the Irish regarded shamrocks as in some way iconic but could hardly believe they actually made tea from them.

Siobhan explained with a laugh. "Yes; only three leaves! That's what we say about weak tea!"

Several 'cups that cheer but not inebriate' were consumed as Christian names were exchanged and fellow feelings discovered and the fact of their being co-religionists revealed.

"Thought you would be a Catholic, of course," Martha commented, "name like yours! Rose not one of us though, was she."

"Oh no, she was Church of England, though times were I had hopes of her - she'd come to Mass with me, you know, when the mood took her, and do all the right things, you know, bless herself with the holy water and genuflect. She seemed to enjoy it. Her own church was St Paul's, just down the road from here, but she didn't go every Sunday; well, really not that very often. But they don't usually, Protestants, do they?"

"Got married there, though, didn't she? Mentioned in the Memorial Service, wasn't it?"

"Yes, that's right indeed," Siobhan agreed. "Ronnie was an atheist and he really wanted to get married in a Registry Office but Rose did say she had to have a church wedding. It was just very quiet; there was me and a few people from Ronnie's side and a colleague of his who was best man and then we all went out to lunch afterwards."

"Knew her husband well, did you? Nice man, was he?"

"Oh yes, he was always polite; quite quiet. Rose never brought him to our flat that much; she used to go out with him and go to his place. He did seem very fond of Rose. I thought it was a pity he was an atheist. But then they never had any children. Rose was thirty-six when they got married and he was older than that."

"Hm! Not considered old, nowadays, but it was then." Martha spoke feelingly. "My mother considered me 'on the shelf' when I was twenty-three and not married — made me feel it, too! Nowadays they wait till their forties!"

"Yes, it's terrible! I can't say I approve at all. It can't be good, having a family so late in life. And they don't even get married, some of them, they go on living in sin even when they've got children!" Siobhan was clearly working towards a fine state of moral indignation and Martha began to hope for an opening to introduce the subject she'd been wracking her brain to find a means to mention.

"True, very true. Entirely agree. That friend of mine you met at the Service, well, graveside, now *her* daughter, married though she was, refused to have *any* children till she was over forty! Mother's a nice, sensible woman, too. Remember her? From Oxford? Came with that chap you said you were surprised to hear was there. Theodore Habgood."

Martha had calculated well. The mention of Ted was enough to raise the temperature of Siobhan's hitherto relatively moderate moral indignation to something approaching white heat and to divert her entirely from the run-of-the-mill subject of modern marriage or lack of it.

"Yes, yes! I *certainly* remember! I couldn't *believe* it! That he had the *nerve* to come to the service! But do you know him?"

"Only by sight. Pointed out to me." Martha gave a dismissive shrug. "Know him by sight yourself, do you?"

"No. I didn't realise he was there until the person by the grave — your friend, is she? — told me. I only know him by repute; and that's more than enough! He's got the most terrible reputation."

"What? Why?"

"He's an appalling womaniser; a serial adulterer — no, a *multiple* adulterer!"

Martha suppressed a smile with some difficulty and managed an expression of suitable shock. "At *his* age?"

"Well, he hasn't always been the age he is now."

Martha acknowledged the truth of this incontrovertible statement and merely enquired "Rose knew him a long time, then?"

"Yes, years ago. When she was married. A friend of hers was going out with that Theodore and they went and stayed with Rose and Ronnie some-times. Then *he* kept going to see Rose on his own; he really went all out after her — and he was a mar-ried man himself — and she had a terrible time getting away from him. In the end Ronnie banned him from the house."

"No, really? Rose tell you, did she?"

"Yes; she used to confide in me all along. She often rang me up when Ronnie was out. Poor Rose, we had long talks on the phone. I wouldn't have thought that Theodore would have dared show his face in that Hampshire village again after what Rose told me."

Martha did not deem it necessary to mention that Ted had visited the village very frequently in re-cent years and visited Rose even more frequently in her flat in Oxford. They continued to converse for some time with reiterated defamation of Ted but without any further information of any new worth being imparted and Martha merely noted that yet another facet of Rose's multiple person-ality had been exposed. She took her leave from Siobhan with compliments, gratitude and mutual amiability.

CHAPTER 22

After a perilous but amazingly unscathed drive back to Oxford, Martha telephoned Mary Ann and arranged to see her the next morning and impart all the information she had gleaned in London. Mary Ann then telephoned her friend Clarissa to ask when she could pass on to her such information as she was about to glean. Clarissa was interested.

"Tell you what," she suggested, "I've got a choir practice in the church tomorrow; why don't you meet me there at the end of it and we can go and have a bite of supper somewhere and talk about it then. Gordon gets his own meal on choir practice nights so I won't need to dash home."

This was eagerly agreed and the following evening the choir practice was briskly taken and finished early. Mary Ann had not yet arrived when it ended. Clarissa and her friend Cedric watched Ted as he left the church: a grey, bent, slightly limping figure, whose clothes looked loose on him and accentuated his aged, shambling appearance.

"Oh dear, poor darling Ted!" Cedric was actually more critical than sympathetic. "He truly does let himself go too dreadfully. One really does not need to go about looking so *boringly* aged!"

"Well, he actually is quite old, you know. My friend Mary Ann's coming in in a minute to impart some news she's been told about him, which she seemed to find exciting rather than boring."

Cedric was all ears. "Gossip, darling? Hot gossip? How I love it! Let me join you. please, *please.* There's been nothing exciting to talk about since the Bee's wedding and that was absolutely *ages* ago. Oh, here's your dear kind informative friend! Mary Ann, darling, I hear you have *news* to impart. Clarissa says I can come with you both and *share* in the excitement!"

"Now really Cedric," Clarissa protested, "I didn't say anything of the sort. But I don't suppose we can stop you if you're determined. Do you mind, Mary Ann?"

Mary Ann was not at all displeased to have her audience increased, even if only by one, especially as Cedric was a most receptive and appreciative one, whose love of gossip was second to nobody's. They all, therefore, walked the few yards to the nearest pub and having bought their drinks settled themselves in a relatively quiet corner.

"Well, let's have it now, Mary Ann, *all* you can tell us about Rose's once-upon-a-time flatmate," Cedric said eagerly, "we're dying for *dire* revelations."

"I don't think there was anything particularly dire about *her*," Mary Ann replied thoughtfully. "She's apparently a rather typical Irish Catholic of the lower - er, respectable um, middle - er,"

"Oh go on, say it Mary Ann, it's one of your favourite phrases, after all, 'lower middle class' is what you mean, isn't it?" Clarissa interrupted.

Mary Ann agreed gratefully and gave a brief description of Siobhan O'Halloran's flat and furnishings as described by Martha. "And she was at Rose's wedding, in an Anglican church; very quiet and not a single member of Rose's family present. She did say Rose had gone to the Catholic church with her sometimes and seemed quite interested, but she was never a Catholic. Martha seemed to think her pretending to be one when she was in Oxford was about the worst thing, but really that was nothing to what she told Siobhan about Theodore. And that was what Martha went to see Siobhan about, why she was so horrified that Theodore was at the Service, even though it was obvious she didn't know him herself." Mary Ann paused for effect and took a large draft of her gin and tonic.

"Well, go on, darling, don't keep us in suspense!" Cedric was enjoying himself.

Mary Ann lowered her voice "She said that Rose had told her he was a serial, no *multiple, adulterer!*"

Cedric and Clarissa both responded by bursting out laughing. They had so recently seen Ted shambling away from choir practice, looking old and bent. They were both a good number of years younger than he was and considered quite ludicrous the idea that anybody as old as that could be capable of such behaviour. This was not exactly the reaction Mary Ann had expected and Clarissa, wiping her eyes and still laughing, explained. "We've just seen him! He looks *ancient!* Surely...."

"Surely," Cedric chimed in, "it's too *utterly* ridiculous!"

"Don't you think so, Mary Ann?" Clarissa asked. "You know what he looks like."

Mary Ann realised that her being much the same age as Ted herself probably coloured her view of him somewhat, but she hastily decided not to admit to this. She hardly hoped to emulate Rose in deleting twelve years from her age, but there was no point in *acting* any older than had become obviously necessary. So she merely replied "Oh, absolutely! He does look frightfully old; and of course I've so often seen him bowed down beneath the weight of other people's bags of shopping that it's hardly helped his image."

"Other people's shopping?" echoed Cedric. "Why, ever?"

"He was very kind and helpful at number nine, you know," Mary Ann admitted. "He did help all of us if we had bags to bring in, anything heavy. I must admit he did kind, helpful things for all of us."

"How marvellous, darling!" said Cedric in tones of apparent sincerity. "If that's the form taken by multiple adultery then clearly it's an activity *entirely* to be recommended!"

The responding laughter was general and Mary Ann was grateful to Cedric and almost relieved, now, that her 'revelations' were having such a comic effect.

Clarissa wondered aloud, however, that Ted's wife Emily was so tolerant of his behaviour with other women. "He must do much more for them than he does for her," she observed. "I've heard her talking about the weight of the shopping she brings home by herself, as well as things there are to be done in the house that don't get done. But she usually ends with a laugh."

"Judging from the amount of time he used to spend at number nine," Mary Ann added, "she can't be used to seeing very much of him."

"But she's not always there, you know," Cedric spoke knowledgeably. "She goes on courses and trips and ever since Bee's wedding she's been staying with her and her husband in Essex from time to time."

"Good heavens, Cedric," Clarissa was amazed, "that's the last thing I would have expected. How on earth do you know?"

"Grapevine, darling, grapevine. People like me who belong to a persecuted minority tend to be on very efficient grapevines."

"You're hardly persecuted these days, Cedric," said

Clarissa dismissively.

"Less so, certainly; but still a minority; and with the ease of modern communications the grapevine's stronger than ever. So I happen to know, and know about, people in Essex — especially a number to do with the Church — whom Emily met up with at Bee's wedding and sees not infrequently. Usually mid-week, though, so you wouldn't realise. She's back in her churchwarden's place in our church on Sundays."

"It's true she never seemed to mind about Bee," Clarissa mused reflectively, "though everybody else was appalled and embarrassed for her. I never could understand it."

"How she can go and *stay* with somebody like Bee is really amazing," Mary Ann voiced her distaste. "Emily's always seemed quite, well, *comme il faut*, and that Bee person can only be described as *loud*!"

"Not only that, darling," Cedric was not averse to having the last word, "I've heard her described as quite a remarkable number of other things!"

Martha made a special trip to Headington to visit Millie and give her the details of her meeting with Siobhan O'Halloran.

"Already knew Rose wasn't a Catholic, of course."

"Oh, I know you explained about her not being married in a Catholic church and how that meant she couldn't be a Catholic, especially back in the 1960s. I don't think any of us knew about that before. I mean, with C.of E people it doesn't matter. But did you find out why her flatmate was so shocked Ted was at the Service in Hampshire?"

"Certainly did. Rose had told her he was a multiple adulterer with a terrible reputation. Tried it on with Rose. Wouldn't leave her alone. Drove her mad. Her husband banned him from the house. Practically from the district!"

Millie was aghast. "But it's impossible! Rose *can't* have told her that!"

"Who else could?" Martha enquired.

Millie had to admit that there seemed to be nobody else. "Unless it was that Rachel Thompson; though she must have known how Ted kept going there and helping Rose to move and everything. So it must have been Rose herself. But I can't believe it. When did she tell her? I mean, how?"

"Rang her up when her husband Ronnie was out. Talked for hours. Quite a talker, wasn't she?"

"Yes. she did talk a lot," Millie admitted. "And she did complain about Ted a bit; nothing like that, though. I think it's terrible. Poor Ted; he'd be so hurt and upset if he knew. Except I can't think he'd believe it. I could never tell him."

"Any better, now, is he? Not so miserable?"

"He does seem a bit more resigned; up and down, though. He's very edgy and goes off the deep end if you say the wrong thing. I told him once he wouldn't have any friends left at all if he didn't mend his ways and his temper. He hasn't been quite so bad since. Emily says she's forever eating left-over food because he cooks at home such a lot and then doesn't eat anything himself. But she ends up laughing about it, like she always does about things."

Millie and Martha had something like a discussion of Emily's behaviour; not that Martha knew her except by one introduction and by repute, but she was interested in her personality, in the psychology behind her seeming lack of reaction, her unusually passive behaviour. She realised that the inappropriate laughter often exhibited was a known psychological phenomenon, originally a defensive mechanism, which was hardly to be wondered at in somebody married to a Ted/Theodore!

The last person to be informed of Martha's findings was Benedicta, whose response was more measured than Millie's or even Mary Ann's. "Rose always did present different faces to different people," she commented, "right from the start when she gave us all different versions of her name. That's how she got on very well with everybody. She did confide in me. I knew how old she was; she didn't mind admitting to eighty-seven when she was speaking to an over-ninety!"

"Knew she wasn't a Catholic, then did you? Surely

not; you got a priest to see her!"

"I think she almost thought she was a Catholic. The priest would have asked her if she wanted to be one and received her on her death bed if she'd said yes. I hope that's what did happen, but it's not for us to know."

Martha was less inclined to be charitable. "Terrible, I think, pretending to be a Catholic just to back up the Spanish myth. Worst thing, I think!"

"Why, what harm has it done?"

"Bad example. Never went to Mass, well, hardly ever. Gave scandal, too, that behaviour with a married man."

Benedicta smiled and sighed. "Most of us are bad examples in some way or another, so we are! But no, the worst thing was to blacken the poor man's name: detraction that is, a black sin, and any gossip's guilty of it. But she did it to diminish the scandal, of course. She couldn't be accused of carrying on with a man she was so rude about, now could she?"

Martha had to admit that that was a possibility, but she could hardly see it as any kind of excuse. Of course she had never actually had more than a couple of conversations with Rose herself and had felt little of the charm that Rose had undeniably possessed and been well able to employ when she had wished to. She had, in fact, felt decidedly rejected by Rose, which was hardly surprising as her knowledge of Spanish would have been considerably greater than any Rose could have acquired in some preliminary study in England and a mere year's stay in Spain. Moreover, Rose had spoken of Argentina when first acquainted with Martha and had clearly been phased by her unexpected knowledge of that country. Neither the claim of an Argentinian nor a Spanish upbringing with an English governess would have stood up to such exposure to a habitual and practised speaker of the language.

"But look now," Benedicta continued, "what harm has she done to anybody but herself? Nobody's told that poor deluded man what she said about him and he wouldn't believe it if they did. The harm's all in himself. He'd no business to be so persistently devoted, and much of it was in his imagination, so it was."

"Set people in the house against each other, though, hasn't she; not to mention that Rachel from Hampshire! And truth! Doesn't truth matter?" Martha was indignant.

Benedicta held up her hands in a dismissive gesture. "Ach," she said, "it's pride and envy that sets people against one another, so the fault's in themselves, so it is."

CHAPTER 23

Eventually the news of Martha's visit to Siobhan O'Halloran permeated even to Marjorie, but she was more concerned with the fact that she missed Rose's company sadly than with any great concern about Rose's earlier life. If she thought about that at all she simply considered that she herself was the one to whom Rose had told the real truth as she herself had undoubtedly been Rose's best friend. She went about sorrowfully like a grieving widow, expressing her distress to anybody who would listen but signally failing to elicit any particular sympathy from her house mates. She did occasionally commiserate with Ted, mainly by telephone, but as each of them was mainly concerned, not to say preoccupied, with their own feelings, their conversational exchanges were not entirely satisfactory.

Rachel Thompson, who had promised to visit Valerie, to have her to stay in Hampshire and maintain their friendship in every possible way, somehow never managed to be available and thus faded from the scene. As their mutual amity had been of short duration and primarily based on nothing very much stronger than a mutual dis-like of 'Theodore', this was not felt at all deeply by Valerie, who was now happily relieved to have her car parking space uninhabited by anybody else and was only mildly exasperated by the noise Martha's car invariably made as she drove in and out of the car park at top speed and with grind-ing gears. This was, she felt, a comparatively very minor source of irritation. Martha clearly knew Benedicta best of their house mates, but she was not close to any of them and had so far aroused no ill feeling in any quarter.

Mary Ann Evans, who still saw Theodore/Ted at church and discussed him — and his wife — with Clarissa and Cedric and sometimes Millie, who seemed to be there more frequently than before, probably maintained more interest in the con-cerned relationships than anybody else in number nine. She went so far as to take Millie to a cham-pagne tea in The Old Parsonage, where they fairly happily went over the details of Martha's revela-tions and Millie expressed her horror at Rose's perfidy and her distress at Ted's devotion to such a woman and her continuing amazement at his wife's apparent lack of concern about it.

"I mean," Millie continued, "where I come from husbands and wives do everything together, well perhaps except going to the pub and football matches, but they go shopping together and they wouldn't go out in the evening without each other, and surely not with anybody else. I know it's different here with University people, but even the ones at their — your — church think the way Ted goes on sometimes is really bad, especially with him not taking any notice of his wife being there. You must have heard them talking about it."

"I have indeed, and even seen it for myself," Mary Ann averred.

"Perhaps Rose really meant something like that when she was talking about him to that Siobhan," Millie said hopefully, "and it just got exaggerated."

"It certainly got exaggerated by *somebody*," Mary Ann agreed grimly. "Our housemate Benedicta, you know, the one who used to be a nun, says that Rose never really did any harm to anybody, but then she always tries to see the good in people. It can be quite tiresome at times, don't you think?"

"What, seeing the good in people?" Millie was a little puzzled.

"Yes, well, saying so, anyway. Of course one knows it's what one *ought* to do, but it does rather put a dampener on the conversation. And Rose can't have done any good to Theodore and Emily, though it's true things were bad enough even before that."

Mary Ann mentally registered the fact that when Millie came to their church Ted always arrived and left with her, though Emily came and went on her own. This, however, was something she did not feel it expedient to mention in the present context, though she did wonder if Millie herself felt any awareness of it. This seemed unlikely as Millie agreed quite heartily that she had often felt very sorry for Emily and even added that she had stuck up for her more than once when Ted had been particularly unpleasant, even rude, to her. Though this was not precisely the kind of behaviour to which Mary Ann had been referring, she was none the less interested and saved up the information to discuss subsequently with her friend Clarissa. In all, she considered that the outing with Millie had been a considerable success. Besides, it was an excellent reason to indulge in a champagne tea.

Mary Ann had agreed to join Clarissa in the church after the choir practice as before, and again Cedric insisted on joining them.

"Now *do* tell me," he said, "that I should know better than to insist on being where I'm not wanted, because if you do I shall have a marvellous opportunity to quote that *incomparable* character Violet Elizabeth Bott and say 'I *like* being where I'm not wanted; it's generally much more interesting than being where I *am* wanted!'"

Clarissa laughed till she wiped her eyes and managed to say "Really Cedric, you are priceless! We'll have to let you come with us after that, won't we

Mary Ann?"

"It's Richmal Compton who's priceless, not me," Cedric disclaimed with unusual modesty. "You must know those wonderful *William* books where Violet Elizabeth Bott lives and breathes and has her being and threatens to 'thcream and thcream till she's *thick*' if she doesn't get her own way!"

"Oh, of course I do; they're still a favourite read and a guaranteed antidote for depression; but it's clever of you to come out with something so apt. So we don't want *you* thcreaming and thcreaming till you're thick, because I'm quite sure that, like Violet Elizabeth, you *can!*"

Clarissa and Cedric went on laughing and Mary Ann, who was also familiar with the *William* books, though less inclined to find the quotations from them so hilariously amusing and somewhat surprised at somebody of Clarissa's academic status doing so, mused on the interesting oddity of the friendship between the two musicians.

They settled at their usual table in the corner of the nearby pub and Mary Ann outlined some details of her champagne tea — "Which of course Millie called *afternoon* tea, but then I suppose one almost has to now" — laying particular stress on Millie's disapproval of Ted's behaviour with and over other women, like Bee and Rose, and her apparent blindness to his attentions to herself even in his wife's presence.

"Oh but, darling," Cedric said immediately, "didn't

you realise that's been going on for positively *years* and *years* and *years!* And poor dear Millie, in between spells of Ted's devotions to Sues and Sarahs and Bees and Roses has recurring turns as what you I'm sure, Mary Ann darling, would term *la favorita..*"

"I don't think *I* quite realised that," was Clarissa's observation, "but then I haven't been here anything like as long as you have, Cedric. How does Millie put up with it and why? It's not as if she's married to him."

"Oh, she copes by being quite *wonderfully* friendly with them all. She works on the 'any friend of Ted's is a friend of hers' line. She was even, to all appearances, a terrific friend of Rose's until that one more or less disappeared into the hospital, and Ted with her."

"That's not quite what I meant," Mary Ann objected. "It was Millie being so sorry for Emily and so shocked about Ted going out with other women and paying them attention in front of his wife, and yet not seeming to have any qualms about his doing the same with *her.* That's what I find so strange."

"Ah, well, it's generally supposed that we don't see ourselves as others see us: 'O wad some power the giftie gie us /Tae see oursels as ithers see us' as Robbie Burns puts it, or something like that. My Scots isn't very accurate, I'm afraid." Clarissa spoke rather feelingly. "Nowadays I think it's called having insight, or some such psychological term. A lack of self knowledge, or rather worse than that, if one doesn't have it. Like an alcoholic refusing to realise that he's got a drink problem."

"Well, personally, darlings, and without any disrespect to dear Robbie Burns, of whom I'm quite passionately fond — such a social rebel — I have absolutely no desire for any 'giftie' to give me *any* notion of how others see me; I'm perfectly content with the way I see myself. I don't in the least want my beautiful vision disturbed."

Cedric smiled at their laughter and Mary Ann remarked that Millie probably had a very similar viewpoint, though she would hardly express it in the same way, or be anything like so well aware of it. "But also," she went on, "I don't think Millie really liked Rose, even before all this falsified background stuff came out. And she's really had to suffer with Ted having something like a breakdown over the death."

"That's probably why she's so indignant about it on Emily's behalf," Clarissa said thoughtfully, "she's transferring her own feelings to Emily, though she doesn't realise it."

"How very right you most probably are, darling," Cedric was, as usual, to have the last word. "It's so very much safer to be desperately indignant for *anybody* else rather than for oneself!"

CHAPTER 24

Millie was expecting Ted to come in for a gin and tonic after his choir practice as he usually did on a Friday at about half past six or seven o'clock. He'd never been later than half past seven and here it was, by her clocks and her watch, almost half past eight! She tried his mobile again (refusing to admit to herself how many times she'd tried it already) and again got only the automatic answer. Finally, at almost a quarter to nine, the front door was heard to respond to an external key and to open accordingly but without the usual accompaniment of "Hullo love, it's me!" She was almost afraid it must be somebody other than Ted when he came into the sitting room looking even more distraught and distressed than he had in all the time since Rose's illness and death. "Oh my God,' Millie agonised to herself, 'somebody's told him the things Rose said to Siobhan about him. Nothing else could make him look like that'.

"Ted!" Millie exclaimed. "Whatever's the matter? You must not take on so! You must realise Rose is dead and gone and whatever you've heard…"

"Rose?" Ted queried. "Rose? I'm not thinking about Rose!"

"Well, you usually are; at least every five minutes, you told me!" Millie's gibe was an unconscious reaction to her apparently misplaced anxiety.

"No." If Ted was aware of the unaccustomed acid in Millie's tone he showed no sign of it. "No. It's Emily. She's gone."

"Gone? Where? What do you mean?"

"She sent me an email. I got it at the office after choir practice. I...I can't...You read it. I've printed it out." Ted handed a slightly crumpled sheet of printed paper to Millie, jolted himself into a chair and put his head in his hands. Unlike his thoughts about Rose his thoughts about Emily clearly 'lay too deep for tears'. Millie straightened the page and read the letter.

Dear Ted,

Only I should put 'dear John' because this is what the Americans call a 'dear John letter'. I'm going to send it just before I leave and I won't be coming back, except in about a month's time, to start collecting the things I want. I've had enough of being the poor little wife who's left at home while you go out with other women; I've had enough of everybody pitying me while you smarm all over somebody else; I've had enough of everybody seeing how you cared for Rose so much and don't care for me at all. I've found somebody who really loves me and we're going away together. I don't suppose you'll bother to try and find me but don't, anyway, because I'll be on the sea. We'll be away a month and when we come back we'll start the divorce proceedings. He's a widower, so no problems there. Then we'll get married and maybe I'll have a real married life with somebody who goes shopping with me and not with other women, and takes me out to restaurants. Somebody who loves me.

So goodbye.

Ex.

Oh dear! I was going to sign it the way you do to your girlfriends, like T.x. But I forgot to put in the dot - which really makes it much more appropriate!

Millie read the letter twice and still found it hard to believe it was real. That Emily, of all people, should have a lover was astonishing enough; that she should go away 'on the sea' with him was too amazing to credit. On the other hand, it could explain much of the passivity of Emily's attitude over the last few weeks and months, of her apparent detachment from Ted and his all too overtly emotional response to Rose's illness and death. It would make some sense if Emily had had other, more interesting things to occupy her mind.

Ted took his hands away from his head, looked at Millie and asked "Well?"

"You didn't have any idea about this at all?" she

knew he hadn't but could think of nothing else to say.

Ted slowly moved his head from left to right as he replied "I never, never thought of anything like it."

"You never did think about how she felt though, did you?"

"She never said."

"You didn't know she was unhappy?"

"I always cooked for her on Saturdays. She liked Rose. She liked you. I thought she didn't want to go to restaurants. She didn't want to drink much."

"She always seemed to enjoy herself when she did come to restaurants with us." Millie stifled some qualms of guilt and repressed the thought that she and Ted had more often been to restaurants *a deux* with Emily left at home.

Ted appeared to feel no qualms of guilt at all. "Yes," he replied, "well, she often did come with us, didn't she? She could have *said* she wanted to come too."

"Oh yes!" Millie's tone was heavy with irony, but irony was not something easily perceived by Ted. "Oh yes! When she knew you only wanted to go with somebody else and she'd be in the way!"

"She didn't know. She didn't mind. She should have said, if she minded. It's not fair! I thought I'd been punished enough with Rose dying, without Emily leaving me as well!" At the mention of Rose Ted's sobs broke out as usual.

This was too much for Millie, who was coming to identify quite strongly with Emily and whose store of sympathy for Ted was almost exhausted.

"Stop talking about being *punished*," she shouted. "Who do you think you are to be specially *punished* by the death of a sick old woman of eighty-nine?"

"Eighty-seven." Even amid his sobs Ted was determined that Rose's age, however advanced, should be remembered accurately.

"Eighty whatever!" Millie shouted again. "It's still old. It's really old. People do die when they're old. And as for you being *punished* by Emily, well, p'raps that's got some truth in it, but really it's because she's found somebody who makes her feel loved and wanted and *happy*, and you didn't. She's gone because she wants to be with *him,* not because she wants to punish *you!*"

Mentally switching from Rose to Emily at least had the effect of stemming Ted's tears. He sat silent in thought for some minutes and then said "I sometimes used to wish she'd find somebody else; it would have made me feel better. But not *go away* with them; not *leave altogether.* I would never do that. I would never have left her. She didn't need to do that. I'd've always been there for her. She should have known that."

"Why should she have known that? She must have often felt you'd dump her and go off with Rose — must have felt she'd been dumped already!"

To Millie's astonishment Ted stood up suddenly and shouted "*Fuck* Rose!"

"I'm sure you did," Millie observed.

"No, I didn't! I told you I didn't! It wasn't like that!"

"Well it's made you lose Emily."

"Yes, that's what I meant. But I didn't — not with Rose — Emily should have known that..."

"Fucking somebody doesn't need to mean much; it's being with them all the time that means a lot more. And that's what you've been doing, all the time, with one woman after another and never with Emily. But Rose was the *end*, the very, very last straw, and now you've lost a sweet-natured, loyal, devoted wife because of the way you've been going on over a deceitful old woman who not only told you lies all the time but told other people lies about you: mean, horrible lies. And you've only got yourself to blame that Emily's left you. It's a wonder she didn't do it long ago. So you can stop feeling aggrieved — and I'm sick of being sorry for you."

Ted said nothing. He lowered his head, raised it slowly, turned and went out of the house slowly and quietly.

CHAPTER 25

Mary Ann Evans was a little held up on her way to church on Sunday morning by Valerie wanting to complain to her about Martha's car. She got away as soon as possible but was rather later than usual and Clarissa had already started playing the organ by the time she arrived. Cedric, however, managed to emerge briefly from the choir vestry and catch her eye as she came in. "Have I got news for *you*!" he mouthed. "See you later!"

As she sat in her accustomed pew Mary Ann noticed that Millie was already sitting in a pew just ahead of her, but when the choir processed in she noticed that Ted was not among its members. That, she thought, was decidedly strange, and she wondered what it might have to do with Cedric's 'news'.

After the service, while the organ was still going full force, Millie went up to Mary Ann and, as they both waited to speak to Clarissa, Mary Ann remarked that she particularly wanted to speak to Cedric "because he saw me just as I came in and managed to say he'd got news for me," she continued.

"So have I," Millie stated rather grimly.

"Oh? Do you know why Emily and Ted are not here?"

"I know why Emily's not here, but I'd hoped Ted might be. I haven't been able to contact him since Friday night. I'm really worried about him."

"Why? What's happened?"

Before Millie could reply Cedric floated up to them and cut in. "*I* can tell you what's happened. Emily's gone off with one of the clergy of Chelmsford Cathedral, that's what's happened!"

"Gone off with somebody? Emily? I don't believe it!" Mary Ann was too completely taken aback to say any more or to stop staring at Cedric. Clarissa came up and joined the group.

"Ah!" she said "I see you've heard the news! But I expect you knew already, Millie."

"Well, I did know Emily had gone, but I didn't know who with. Ted didn't either."

"It's somebody she's been seeing in Essex lately," Cedric informed them with relish. "One of the Cathedral clergy. He's a friend of Bee's husband, that's how she met him. Ironical, don't you think?"

Mary Ann recovered her voice. "I know you said Emily had been staying with Bee and her husband recently — but no, I can't believe it; she was so quiet, so *docile,* so un...un...un*likely!*"

"Ah, well 'Still waters run deep, my dear,'" Cedric quoted.

"'There's no smoke without fire!'" Clarissa finished the quotation for him and they laughed. "Not," she added, 'that I'd ever suspected even the most *minute* flame to be burning in that quarter. And I'd never detected a whiff of smoke till you told us about the visits to Essex the other day."

"Well, of course it was very noticeable there, but almost nothing was likely to make it apparent here."

Millie, who had been a little lost during the exchange of quotations, was at least up to the implication of 'visits to Essex'. "It's true Emily's been away quite a lot during the week; but she often did used to go on trips by herself or with her daughter so I never thought that much about it."

"When did Ted find out? He seemed no worse than usual at choir practice on Friday," Clarissa wanted to know.

"He called in at his office after that on his way back to Headington and found an email from Emily. He printed it out and then brought it round to show me. She said she was going away with somebody who really loved her; *her,* not other people, and it was no use Ted trying to find them because they'd be on the sea and not back for a month. And then she'd start divorce proceedings and come back for the things she wanted."

"That was brief and to the point, anyway, even if she didn't say who she was going with." Mary Ann was no longer incredulous. "But I'm even more surprised it's a *clergyman*, I mean. one wouldn't expect..."

"Clergymen can behave every bit as badly as anybody else, darling," was Cedric's immediate comment. "I should know!"

Clarissa laughed but Millie and Mary Ann looked even more shocked. Cedric smiled at them benignly as he added "Don't be upset, darlings, this one's not so very bad at all; he's a widower, so it's only one little bit of adultery, not two."

Millie, who had come to Ted's church largely in the hope that he would be there, hurried back to Headington to make another determined effort to see him at his house. Previously she had only telephoned and, that failing, knocked long and loud at both front and back doors. This time, worried for Ted's safety, she took the spare key from its hiding place in the coal shed and opened the back door. She went in, calling Ted's name as she did so. Finally, when she had looked into every room on the ground floor and was going up the stairs, she heard his answering voice.

"All right," it called, "hang on." As Millie reached the top of the stairs Ted, wearing a very crumpled nightshirt, emerged from the main bedroom. Millie's relief expressed itself in exasperation.

"For heaven's sake, Ted. Pull yourself together and

get dressed and come downstairs!" Ted hesitated, looked a little dazed, said nothing and disappeared into the bedroom.

"I'm going to put the kettle on," Millie shouted, "I'll see you dressed and downstairs by the time I've made a cup of tea. Or *else!*" she finished.

Millie's years of dealing with difficult patients in a doctor's practice in the days when doctors' receptionists had some clout, stood her in good stead. Sympathetic concern might have met with resistance; peremptory command was complied with. She was putting the tea on the table when Ted, unkempt and unshaved but dressed in shirt and trousers, came into the kitchen. Millie poured his tea the way he liked it with liberal amounts of milk and sugar and set it before him as he sat at the table.

"You weren't at church this morning," she stated.

"How do you know?" Ted asked.

"I didn't suppose you'd go in your nightshirt, did I?"

"I mean, is that why you've come round now? How did you know I wasn't there?"

"Because I went there myself, of course."

"You can't have thought I'd go there."

"Why not? You've always been before."

"I don't want anybody to see me."

"No, I don't suppose you do, looking the way you do now." Millie maintained her resolution to show disapproval rather than sympathy. "You can't go on like this; it doesn't make sense. You didn't mind people seeing you when you were wallowing in grief over Rose and getting yourself banned from the hospital; why don't you want people to see you now?"

Ted sat silent and stared past Millie at the opposite wall. Millie waited for a full minute and then said "Well?"

Ted gave a long sigh, looked down at the surface of the table and finally muttered: "Too ashamed."

Mary Ann could hardly wait to get back to number nine and relay the information of Emily's departure from the matrimonial home, not to mention the accustomed church! Once at home, however, she decided that lunchtime was hardly the best time for the immediate dissemination of so interesting a piece of news, so she merely invited everybody by telephone to come and have coffee and a 'tiny drink' with her after lunch as she had something to tell them. Nobody could resist so interesting an invitation and by two-thirty Valerie, Benedicta, Martha and Marjorie were all assembled in Mary Ann's drawing room with cups of strong coffee and small glasses of some interesting liqueurs.

"Well, Mary Ann," Valerie was the one to enquire, "you must have heard something at that church you go to these days."

"It seems quite a well-spring of local information," Marjorie added. "We can see why you go!"

"It's just this," Mary Ann was beginning to fear that her information would fail to be as interesting to the assembled company as she had initially supposed, so she decided to play it down. "It's, well, it might be considered the final episode of the story of our former house mate Rose; her *cavalier servente* has been dumped by his wife and she's gone off with a clergyman from Chelmsford Cathedral, a friend of that Bee woman's husband. She left him on Friday and sent an email telling him not to try and find her because she and her *inamorato* will be on the sea for the next month!"

Marjorie was not merely the most astonished but the first to reply. "I can't *believe* it!" she gasped. "Such a meek woman! We were all so sorry for her! I could never have *imagined...*!"

"Well good for her!" was Valerie's contribution. "I've wondered about her ever since Rose first arrived and we were all waited on by that Theodore when she had us round to drinks. He was talking about his wife then while he was waiting on Rose hand, foot and finger at the same time. You knew her, though, didn't you Marjorie. What was she like?"

"Nobody could really make her out. Ted used to behave outrageously at things like college dinners, making up to other women and talking about his girlfriends in boasting tones. It was terribly embarrassing."

"And his wife there all the time?" Martha queried.

"He was like that at the church things, too," Mary Ann added, "especially with that Bee person. His wife never seemed too phased by it. It was very strange. Sometimes she'd just laugh. And then we heard lately that she was really friendly with Bee and used to go and stay in Essex with her and her husband. I did think that was surprising; Bee was really — well, I mean Emily was always quite refined, which Bee certainly was not!"

"But now Emily's found herself a lover; somebody she met through Bee!" Valerie, always on the side of wronged and slighted women, was positively triumphant.

"Not to mention that Bee's an excellent role model when it comes to getting rid of unsatisfactory husbands!" Mary Ann added. "She must have been very encouraging."

Martha was less inclined to approve. "Broken marriage, though, whatever you say! Eh, Benedicta?" Martha sought the agreement of the only other Catholic but was also motivated by the desire to show that Rose had been a more harmful influence on others than Benedicta had seemed willing to admit. "Can't say now that Rose never really did anybody any damage!"

Marjorie, though perhaps more sympathetic to Ted than any of the others, was still loath to lay too much blame on her dear departed friend. "I don't think you can blame Rose," she asserted immediately. "What about Bee? Not to mention a succession of similar women?"

"That's probably the point," Valerie spoke convincingly, "the others *were* similar, and they were very much here today and gone tomorrow. A wife can cope with that. She knows they won't last; they won't be around for long. Rose wasn't merely the last but the *lasting* straw! Bad enough that she'd been a perpetual presence for years commanding devoted attention, she didn't fade from the scene even after she'd died! It must have been worse than ever. There's nothing like dying to make somebody immortal!"

"Now really," Mary Ann objected, "that *is* a contradiction!"

"No, indeed it's quite right you are, Valerie," Benedicta spoke firmly. "The saints become saints only after they're dead; the dead can be venerated with their virtues to the fore and their imperfections forgotten. That poor man's been making a saint out of a very fallible woman with all his overgrieving. We see it often; a mother loses a child and all her other children suffer because the dead can do no wrong and the living can never be so perfect as she imagines the departed child to be! That sort of grieving is a great danger, so it is! It's a kind of addiction and likely to be just as hard to cure. But with all her stories about herself Rose never made out she was a saint! She wanted to please people, to be sure, she showed each one a side of her she knew they wanted to see. Indeed she was not quite honest; but can she be blamed for a fool man trying to make a saint out of her after she's dead and so driving his wife away?"

Benedicta's words were received with silence. There was nobody who disagreed and the gathering changed in tone from a superficial sharing of gossip to a more profound sense of the problems of human nature and the workings of human society.

At last Mary Ann spoke. "You're wiser than the rest of us, Benedicta. Most of us see things in a personal, judgmental, superficial way; you see to the core of things. You see life clearly and see it whole. We should take notice of you. We'd all be the better for it."

EPILOGUE

The shock of Emily's departure and the reality of it at least had the salutary effect of diverting Ted from his grief over Rose. When the divorce was finalised Emily married her clergyman. They had quite a sizeable wedding in Chelmsford Cathedral and a number of people from Ted's church attended. Ted had approved thoroughly of twice-divorced Bee's third church wedding but he felt very differently about the one involving his ex-wife. He was in fact invited but unsurprisingly refused to attend, although their daughter acted as bridesmaid.

His relationship with Millie went on in very much the same way as before, except that he cooked for her on a Saturday evening as he could no longer do it for Emily. He did eventually ask her to marry him but Millie was a great deal too sensible to do anything of the sort. She valued her independence and her ability to furnish her own house the way she wanted it without interference. She was, moreover, well aware that the status of a frequent companion was greatly to be preferred to that of a very infrequently accompanied wife.

Emily's second marriage was extremely happy; feeling exclusively loved and wanted she acquired a confidence she had never previously possessed. Her husband lacked Ted's ability to cook but was immensely appreciative of the food Emily provided for him and Emily was delighted to cook just what she herself enjoyed without having to spend the best part of every week consuming, alone, the surplus of Ted's Saturday dinners. After some four years, however, a heart attack dispatched Emily's husband with unexpected suddenness. Ted hastened to comfort her and was soon paying her almost as much diligent attention as he had shown to Rose. It was accepted with a resigned lack of enthusiasm, which might not have been the best way of ensuring its continuance. This was, however, fortuitously achieved when Emily fell off a ladder and broke her hip, thus rendering her an even more necessitous object of Ted's concern. They never actually married again but continued much as if they had never been divorced, a state of affairs quite mutually satisfactory.

News of this situation filtered through to the occupants of number nine through the good offices of Mary Ann Evans, who was dismissive of Emily's 'ridiculous weakness'. Valerie, however, who was now spending most of her days and a good many nights looking after her ex-husband since he had been disabled by a stroke and deserted by his mistress, shrugged philosophically and observed that marriage might not mean as much as it should but divorce didn't always mean a lot either. Benedicta, who though several years older was none the less wise, pronounced that that was just as it should be, so it was.

!

ACKNOWLEDGE-
MENTS

My heartfelt thanks are due to Joanna Frank, without whose patient help and encouragement I would never have been able to publish anything, and now she has succeeded in sending my third book into orbit.

Many thanks and much appreciation to my granddaughter, Mary Bowen, who created the expressive cover, and to members of my family who read the book as I finished it and were so kind as to deem it worthy of publication.

ABOUT THE AUTHOR

Elizabeth Longrigg

Elizabeth Longrigg has lived for many years in Oxford where she raised her five children. She has taught English Literature at several Oxford colleges and her former students include Philip Pullman, Tina Brown and Val McDermid.

BOOKS BY THIS AUTHOR

The Oxford Pot

The Incident

Printed in Great Britain
by Amazon